# Shadow's Price

### Danni Williams

Dragon Flight Media

# Contents

# Chapter One

The door to the house stood wide open. That was odd. Her brother rarely left the door unlocked, much less left it open.

Sheila shut off the engine of her car and stared at her brother's trailer home. She could see the ceiling fan whirl through the window. The parked cars of her parents and brothers covered the front yard. Nobody in this trailer park had a driveway.

Despite the 110 degree temperature outside and it being almost the same stifling temperature inside her car with the AC going in and out, a shiver racked her body, and goosebumps raised along her dark brown skin. Something was off.

Her wolf growled within her. It sensed something about the scene that it didn't like. Music from the trailer sounded faint inside her car. She opened the door and stepped out.

The coppery, sweet smell of blood assaulted her nose. The wind intermingled the smell with the dusty scents of the desert, making it hard to tell where it came from. She wrinkled her nose in disgust.

Sheila looked around the street to see if she could identify the source of the blood. There was no living creature outside on the street. If it wasn't for the other dilapidated trailers on the street and wrecks of cars, she wouldn't think a soul lived within miles.

"What the hell?" she muttered under her breath. She sniffed the air and swore again. The blood smell came from the trailer.

Pushing down her trepidation, Sheila walked into the trailer. And straight into a nightmare. The doorway opened right into the living area of the home.

Blood was everywhere—the walls, carpet, and furniture. But that wasn't the worst part.

The source of the blood was her family. Her mother and father were lying on the floor, their throats ripped out. Her older brother, Thomas, was sitting at the dinette, his head resting on it. Blood pooled on the surrounding tabletop.

A groan caught her attention. Her younger brother was on the floor near the entrance to the tiny kitchen.

Sheila rushed over to him. "Dave! What happened?"

Dave, her younger brother by five years, opened his eyes.

"Sheila! You've gotta get out of here!" he gasped.

She knelt beside him. He was holding his hands over his stomach. Blood coated them, and it looked as if someone had shot him.

"My God! Who did this?" Sheila was trying her hardest not to faint. The overwhelming, coppery smell nearly had her vomiting. Who wanted to execute her family like this?

"Dennis." He shook his head and coughed. "I'll heal. Dad stole from him."

She put a hand over her mouth in dismay. How could her dad have the balls to steal from one of the biggest crime lords in the Supernatural world? That was just suicidal.

"Go! Dennis said that he would take you as a mate for repayment."

Her wolf, who had been growling inside of her throughout all of this, started howling. It knew that Dennis was bad news.

Dennis was the head of one of the deadliest packs in the southwest. Every member of his wolf shifter pack was a member of his criminal enterprise.

The rumors around the Supernatural community had him killing his last three mates after they failed to give him cubs. Sheila did not want to become mate number four.

"I can't leave you."

Dave's eyes flashed yellow, his wolf peeking out. "You can't do anything for me. Leave. Plan Z."

Plan Z was the code the family used to call for a total evacuation. Her dad had drilled into the entire family how to escape and disappear at a moment's notice. Even though she didn't follow in her family's criminal footsteps, she still prepared to leave.

Tears formed in her eyes. "But..."

"Go! He's looking for you." Dave closed his eyes, his energy spent. "I'll find you once it's safe."

Thirty minutes later, Sheila pulled into a junkyard. She parked in the shade of a trailer just inside the gate.

A man stepped out of the door and walked over to her car. He was a human man, whose skin was bronzed and wrinkled from years in the sun. He looked as if he was in his late 60s or 70s.

"How can I help you, young lady?" He turned and spat into the dirt.

"I need a fresh start. And fast." Her voice was clipped. She was not in the mood to be chatty. Her head was throbbing, and she wished she was elsewhere.

He shaded his eyes with his hand. Her brusqueness didn't bother him. "Come inside." He turned and headed back for the door.

Sheila went to the trunk, pulled out her go bag, and set it by her feet. Then, she lifted the false bottom of the trunk. Where the spare tire sat was a thick, manilla envelope. She pulled it out and dropped it into her bag. After closing her bag, she turned and entered the trailer.

Cool air blasted over her heated skin. She sighed in relief as she cooled off.

The man had seated himself behind a battered, old metal desk. She wondered, with the small part of her mind not filled with grief, if that thing had been around since the last World War.

"Sit down." The man waved at the chair in front of the desk. After she sat, he stared at her. "I've got two untraceable vehicles. One, though, is a junker."

Sheila sighed. This would not be cheap. "And the other?"

"Will get you where you have to go."

She held up the keys to her current car. "I'll take the better one. You'll get rid of the one outside?"

"Yep. It will be stripped and crushed within the hour."

The two haggled for a few minutes before she handed over fifty grand from the manilla envelope in cash. That money had been a gift from her parents when she turned eighteen. She thought it was for college until her mother crushed her hopes by telling her it was only for emergencies. And both of her parents would check at random times to make sure she had touched none of the money.

The man walked out to grab the vehicle. Two minutes later, a horn sounded.

Sheila walked out to see him standing beside a black, late-model Ford Explorer. At any other time, she would have taken the time to admire it. But she was eager to get on the road. So, all she did was a quick run around the vehicle. It had Florida license plates on it.

"Now, those plates won't stand up to too much scrutiny. So, avoid attracting the attention of the police, and get new plates once you get to where you're going."

Sheila nodded and accepted the keys from him. She planned on ditching the ride once she found a place to hide.

She thanked the old human and got into the SUV. The insides were all done up with a crem leather interior. The latest electronics filled the dashboard. Nice.

Her nose wrinkled at the faint smell of old cigarette smoke in the truck. Someone had attempted to deodorize the smell out of it, but her wolf's senses could still tell it was there.

Turning on the Explorer, she checked the gas gauge. The tank was full. Good, she wouldn't have to stop for gas soon.

She automatically reached for her phone and swore as she remembered she tossed it into a trashcan after running it over.

"Note to self, get a prepaid phone at the next stop," she muttered under her breath as she turned the radio on to a local R&B station. A love song came out of the speakers.

Sheila shifted the car into drive and left the junkyard behind after a long look at her old car.

# Chapter Two

A week later, after making several detours through different states, Sheila found herself at a dingy motel in Cleveland. The trip had been long and lonely, but relatively uneventful. There had been no signs that Dennis had followed her.

She had been in town only one day. Long enough to buy an old, crappy tablet off the Facebook marketplace and to get some groceries.

Presently, she was chomping on an apple while looking for a job. She couldn't risk looking for work in her old field of accounting. That would be one of the first things that Dennis's goons would look for.

Her eyes stopped at lists on a local job board. *Waitress needed at the Howling Wolf.* Sheila snorted at the name. She wondered if the bar was owned by a wolf shifter. With a name like that, it wouldn't surprise her.

It was a little after seven. Maybe she could go check it out and apply in person.

While she wished she could wait a few days to get the lay of the land, there just wasn't much money left. She had been afraid to touch the little left in her checking account. Dennis might have someone monitoring all of her financial activity.

The same thing applied to her email and social media. It sucked majorly because she had no one to talk to, and she was lonely.

Oh, how she wished she could call her mom. While she didn't agree with her family's lifestyle, she still loved them.

Blinking back tears, Sheila changed into the last clean outfit she had. One that she had bought at a local superstore on her drive to Cleveland.

It was a nice pair of jeans with a dressy, blue blouse. Perfect for a late summer evening in Cleveland.

Muggy heat assaulted her as she stepped out of the motel. She could feel her hair trying to revert to its natural, curly state in the humidity.

*How in the hell do people survive in this heat?* In Las Vegas, it was just dry heat and dust.

She quickly got into her truck and blasted the air conditioning.

Twenty minutes later, she was standing in front of a door with a sign that read The Howling Wolf in neon-blue lettering. From the music and other sounds she could hear, the bar was on the second floor of the building.

It was a Thursday night, so there was no wait to get in. Just inside the door, a large man sat on a stool.

He was a tall, white man with a bald head and tattoos around his muscled arms. A quick sniff informed Sheila that he was a wolf shifter.

Yep, the place had to be owned by a shifter. Great, that meant she would come to the attention of the local Alpha sooner than later. She would have to find out who the Alpha was in a hurry so that they didn't think she was a rogue.

The bouncer eyed her suspiciously. He had pegged her already as a wolf.

"How may I help you, young lady?" He pitched his voice only loud enough to be heard over the music and street noise. Hopefully, he wasn't the type that attacked those outside of his pack without reason.

Sheila put on a smile that she didn't feel. "I'm here to apply for the waitressing job."

The bouncer relaxed and smiled. "Are you new in town?"

"Yes, I just got here yesterday. I saw the ad, and here I am."

"Go upstairs and tell the bartender you're here about the job." He made a shooing motion with his hands and then turned to the door. A pair of clearly tipsy human women were approaching.

Sheila looked back at the drunk duo and then headed up the stairs.

At the top of the stairs, it opened up to a small room that had a bar running along one side, a few small tables with chairs in the middle, and two booths on the other side. That surprised her since it looked like the bar would be far larger from the outside.

A human couple currently occupied only one booth, enjoying dinner and drinks.

Sheila's stomach growled, reminding her that an apple would not cut it for dinner.

A woman who appeared to be in her late twenties or early thirties was cleaning glasses behind the bar. Sheila went over to her. The bartender set the glass and rag down on the wooden countertop.

"What can I get you?" she asked with a friendly smile. Her green eyes flashed in the light.

"I'm here to apply for the waitressing position." Sheila tried not to take a deep sniff to identify what the bartender was. The smells of food, alcohol, and cigarette smoke kept her from smelling the woman's race.

"That was fast. The boss just put the ad up this morning. I'm Lena." The woman held out a manicured hand that sported dagger-like red nails.

Sheila grabbed her hand and shook it. That brought the woman close enough to smell that she was also a wolf shifter.

"I'm Sheila. I just arrived in town yesterday."

Lena leaned over the bar and spoke in a lower voice. "You're in luck. Brody is our local Alpha, and he owns this bar. He's in tonight, so you can let him know you're in town."

Wolf protocol strongly suggested that visitors from other Packs make themselves known to the local Pack once they arrived. With Sheila practically being a rogue, she would need permission to stay in Cleveland.

*Well, I might as well get this over with.*

"Thank you."

Lena pointed to a barstool. "Have a seat. I'll be right back."

Sheila studied Lena as she left from behind the bar and disappeared through a door in the back.

Lena couldn't have been any more than five feet tall, although when she stood behind the bar she seemed taller.

She had very curly, red hair that hung a little past shoulder length, alabaster skin, and green eyes.

A minute later, Lena stepped back into the bar, followed by an absolute giant of a man.

Sheila could feel his power from across the room. This man was clearly an Alpha. Her eyes widened in surprise. Surely the two humans eating in the booth could feel his power.

But the humans remained oblivious. *Huh.*

The Alpha nodded, and then the outpouring of power stopped.

So that outpouring was just for her benefit.

Brody motioned for her to join him. She followed him into the short hallway. When the door closed, the sound deadened.

*He must've spent a fortune on soundproofing,* she thought as she followed him into an office that was immediately to the right.

"Have a seat."

There was a single chair in front of the wooden desk in the room. The office was sparsely furnished with no decorations. There wasn't even a computer or a filing cabinet. Sheila had the feeling that the Alpha's actual work was done elsewhere.

After seating themselves, the pair sat in silence for a moment, studying each other. From the resemblance to Lena, Brody was her father or uncle. He had the same light skin and red hair. But he was large, nearly seven feet tall, and built like a linebacker.

Sheila wished he would say something. The waiting was wearing on her nerves.

Finally, he spoke. "What is your full name and Pack? We don't have many wolves from southern lines coming through our territory."

Southern lines referred to Black wolves. There weren't many wolf shifters in the United States who were black. All of them could trace their heritage back to Africa.

Under the weight of his green gaze, Sheila found herself telling the truth instead of her carefully prepared lie. "Sheila Davis. I don't have a pack."

Fuck! The Alpha would probably kick her out of his territory. Most Packs didn't like dealing with wolves who didn't belong to a pack.

And for good reason, most wolves without packs were rogues. Just like her family. Or non-conformers who couldn't fit in with the pack mentality.

But all Brody did was just nod. "Are you looking to stay in Cleveland?"

She swallowed nervously. "If I can. I'm looking for a fresh start."

There was that damn phrase again. Fresh start.

Brody's green eyes bored into hers. Sheila wanted to look away, but she couldn't. "Who are you running from?"

The question was so unexpected; she tried to think of a salable answer that would satisfy the Alpha, but all she could do was blink.

"Huh?"

Her wolf twitched inside her, and it clearly wanted Sheila to tell the Alpha the entire sordid tale.

"Someone clearly has you running scared if you're in my territory without family." Brody leaned forward, his voice taking on a note of command.

Sheila's family had carefully kept her away from any Alphas her entire life. If they hadn't, she would have recognized what Brody was doing with his power and fought it.

Despite not wanting to blow her cover, Sheila explained, "Alpha Dennis of the Gamboni Pack is after me because of something that my father did."

The horror of finding most of her family dead finally broke through the wall she had placed around her emotions, and she started crying.

Brody got up from behind his desk and came around to her. He gently helped her up from her chair and wrapped her in a big hug.

That was her undoing. For the first time in over a week, she felt safe enough to grieve.

They stood there for about ten minutes while Sheila cried, and Brody rubbed her back. He didn't stop until she pulled away.

"Thank you." Sheila's voice was hoarse from crying.

Brody looked down at her with sympathy. "Tell me what happened. Maybe we can come to a solution."

Over the next hour, Sheila relayed the story of what happened to her family and her flight across the county to escape from Dennis. She could tell that Brody was getting upset by what she told him.

"What made you break and go straight? Why not follow the rest of your family?" Brody asked as she got to the end of her story.

Sheila sighed. "I hated having to be constantly on alert and hide myself away. We moved often when I was younger when things got too hot for us in an area." She shifted in her chair uncomfortably before continuing.

"Someone in my household was always in jail. Once I stayed with a lion shifter family while both my mom and my dad were in lockup."

She trailed off, remembering the year she spent with them. It had been lovely to be with a stable family. She had attended school, had friends, and she had run with the cubs from their Pride.

"My foster family wanted me to stay with them, but my parents insisted I come back to them. We left the state two days later and ended up in Nevada."

Brody nodded. "I've reached a decision."

Hope and dread fought inside of her, causing Sheila to feel sick to her stomach.

"You can stay in Cleveland for six months on a trial." He held up a hand. "During that time, you will work here on the shifter side of the bar and agree to abide by Pack law. You will also be expected to take part in Pack life. At the end of six months, if you do well and fit in with my Pack, we would expect you to join."

Sheila couldn't believe what she was hearing. He was letting her stay in his territory and letting her join the Pack? Her wolf yapped happily inside her mind.

"Uh, thank you!" She gave him a look of pure gratitude.

He smiled back. "Thank me by working hard and keeping out of trouble."

"I will, sir."

"Good. You'll be staying in the apartment building where most of our young and single wolves live before finding their own accommodations. There will be no rent during your trial."

That would give her plenty of time to save up for a new place.

"Pack tithes are 10% of your wage. Since you work for one of my businesses, tithes to support the pack will be taken out of your check."

The next few minutes passed by in a blur for Sheila as the Alpha called for a few of the pack members to grab her things from the motel and move her truck. Then, Brody led her down the hallway to another set of doors that led to a surprise.

There was another club and bar on the same level. Sheila blinked when she saw the room full of Supernaturals.

"This is the shifter side. The club takes up the most second, third and fourth floors," said Brody as he led her across the floor to a set of elevators. "The fourth floor is for members only."

Sheila looked around, trying not to feel overwhelmed. The waitresses, she noted, wore slinky black dresses or really short shorts with low-cut tops.

*I need to go shopping.*

# Chapter Three

**O**ne Month Later

*Crack!* The glass of blood in Xavier's hand shattered as he heard the words coming out of his phone. Blood dripped onto the gleaming, glass top of his desk.

Xavier looked down at his hand and shook his head in disgust. "Did I hear you correctly? Some unknown wolf shifters dare attack one of my Court? In my fucking territory?"

The voice belonging to his second, Damien, growled back over the phone, "Yes. Penny had been left for dead."

The door to his office opened, and his very human assistant, Anita, looked in. Her face had concern written all over it.

Xavier motioned at the mess he made. She nodded and disappeared. A minute later, she was back, coming in and cleaning up the mess.

"What's worse is that Penny believes that there was a Nightshade or Magician with them."

Fucking great. Someone was either making a move on his territory or the local wolf pack. Or both.

He really didn't need this complication right now. Not with the Mad King of Europe going after the Nightshade Courts of the North American vampires.

"Dammit. Contact Brody and see if he's free to meet tonight." Xavier took a towel from Anita and cleaned his bloody hands.

"He sent me a text a few minutes ago asking to meet at nine." Damien's voice was grim. "I suspect he's got similar news."

"Where?"

"Upper level of The Howling Wolf."

Two hours later, Xavier and his two guards were walking through the tunnel that led from the Moonrise Hotel to the building that housed The Howling Wolf.

The tunnel had been dug so that the Supernatural clientele of The Howling Wolf could come and go without being seen. No one wanted the humans to know who frequented the establishment.

It was extremely vital that the humans didn't know that the CEO of Silver Technologies wasn't human. That would upset them too much and cause him a lot of unneeded stress. Plus, it would have Andre up his ass.

One thing that he learned from growing up in the Silversbane Court was to keep your profile low amongst the humans. Although, as one of Cleveland's richest businessmen, it was hard to stay low profile.

A wolf shifter was waiting at the elevators that led up to the club. He gave a respectful nod to Xander. "Welcome, Mr. Silversbane. The Alpha passes his greetings and asks that you join him on the fourth floor."

Xavier gave him a genuine smile. "How's Susanna settling into college?"

The man gave him a wide grin. "She's loving it. She's making new friends."

"Good. She did great over the summer. My project lead has threatened mutiny if she doesn't come back to work for me next spring."

"I'll let her know that." The teen was gifted when it came to programming. She impressed him so much over the summer that he picked up her tuition at the University of Michigan. Also, the teen wolf had no idea that she had met her Bond mate in another vampire—his second in command.

Luckily for Susanna, she wouldn't feel the pull of their bond for a few years yet. Shifters physically matured slower than humans, so her side of the bond wouldn't kick in until her twenty-first birthday.

The door to the elevator opened, and Xavier and his men entered. The elevator unexpectedly opened on the second floor.

And Xavier's dream stepped inside. A short, beautiful, black wolf shifter entered the elevator. She was trying to balance a laptop bag and a box full of files.

Xavier noted that the mystery lady wore the uniform of a club waitress. Her uniform was a little black dress that left nothing to the imagination.

She accidentally bumped back into him, and he felt a flash of power when they touched.

"I'm so sorry." Her husky voice made the apology seem as if she were reading porn. Or at least, that was what his dick thought.

"You have nothing to apologize for." Xavier couldn't resist and gripped her shoulder to study her.

The zap of power that hit him when he touched her felt like he had stuck a finger in an electrical socket. It was clear that the wolf felt it as well, as her mouth formed a silent "O."

Xavier looked down at the top of her head. She only came up to his shoulder. He wondered what her real hair looked like under the blond wig she wore.

Ignoring the shocked glances of his guards, he reached and took the box of files from her.

"I have them, sir!" she protested. Xavier chuckled softly but didn't give the files back.

The elevator stopped again, this time on the fourth floor. When the door opened, Xavier motioned for the embarrassed wolf to exit.

She gave him a suspicious look, as if she was trying to figure out his motive. He gave her a nod.

He wanted to see her ass, plain and simple. He had gotten an eyeful of her large breasts when she walked in. She turned and walked out of the elevator, and yep, her little black dress showed her tight ass off to perfection.

Xavier followed her into the private lounge. The room was decorated with the theme of an old gentleman's club.

The wolf headed for a booth toward the far end of the floor, where an older lion shifter sat. He recognized him immediately. The shifter owned an investment firm that was headquartered at the Tower.

Once his wolf greeted the lion shifter, she turned back to him. "Thank you, sir, for your help." She reached out to take the box from him.

"My pleasure." Xavier gave her a winning smile before turning to head to the table, where Damien waited for him.

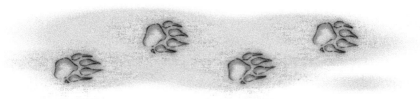

Xavier was sipping on a nice blood wine and talking with Damien, while part of his mind was thinking of the beautiful, young wolf from the elevator. The last thing he wanted to do was to have a meeting. His time would be better spent getting to know the young woman.

He looked up in surprise when the wolf Alpha joined them. By the grim look on the wolf's face, whatever had held him up wasn't good.

"Sorry for my tardiness." Brody sat down. He turned slightly in his seat, looking for someone.

One of the two waitresses on the floor noticed and headed for them.

"Would you like anything else before we start?"

Damien held up his glass. "Another blood wine for me."

"Same for me." Xavier drained the last of his and set the glass down so that the waitress could take it.

The waitress quickly brought back their drinks and departed.

Brody placed a small, green crystal on the table, and all sounds from the room around them faded away. The crystal held a sound dampening spell in it. No one outside of their table could hear their conversation.

"I was late because I received a report about one of my Pack members being harassed by some wolves from another pack." Brody's eyes flashed to the yellow of his wolf's.

That wasn't good. It had to connect back to the attack on Penny. Why was some unknown Pack causing trouble in his territory?

"That makes two attacks so far by unknown wolves." And if they didn't figure out who was behind them, there would be more. "Who is stupid enough to come here and attack us?" Damien's voice was barely above a growl.

Brody's lips twisted as if he tasted something sour. "I have an idea." He looked across the room, and Xavier followed his gaze.

He was staring at the waitress that he met in the elevator.

The woman who was his Shadow. What in the world did she have to do with the attacks? And where did she come from?

"Who?" Xavier knew that his voice sounded rough.

Brody turned his attention back to his guests. His green eyes were as hard as agates. "A rogue Alpha Dennis Gabonine. His Pack is out of the Southwest and is pure Underground."

*Why in the hell is an Alpha from the Southwest challenging an Alpha from the Midwest?* Xavier narrowed his eyes.

"Why would this soon to be dead idiot pick Cleveland?" demanded Damien.

"Because I have something that he wants." Brody's eyes flickered back over to the table where the waitress sat with the lion. She was showing him something on her laptop.

"Does it have to do with your lovely waitress over there?" Xavier nodded in the table's direction where the object of his baser desires sat.

Brody sighed. "Yes. She's hiding from him. Her father stole from Dennis, and he retaliated by killing her entire family."

Anger surged through Xavier at the mention of the threat to his Shadow. For a second, a red mist filled his vision before he clamped it down. Letting anger rule him would cause nothing but problems. He took in a deep breath, willing his emotions back into a box.

He noticed his second giving him a sidelong glance. Damn, his anger must have shown.

"I did a background check on Sheila when she arrived." Brody eyed him warily. "While her entire family was into criminal activity, she wasn't. She was an insurance broker."

The sight of her laughing at something the lion shifter said caught Xavier's attention. His breath caught at the sight. Damien leaned slightly over the table. "Is she worth going to war over?"

"I gave her my word that she could stay in my territory." Brody's voice was very low. "I will not let some criminal asshole come into my territory and harm my own."

The grin that Damien gave Brody was bloodthirsty. Damien was still upset by the attack on Penny. "Good."

"In the past month, she's integrated well with the pack and has been helping those with small businesses get their finances in order." The alpha nodded over at her. "She is fitting in with the Pack."

Xavier cleared his throat. "You should know, she's my Shadow." The words just slipped out without thought. Well, damn, his subconscious picked up on her status faster than the rest of him.

As his Shadow, the young wolf was the one being that was his soul mate. Hecate only granted the Nightshade one Shadow. Once they were Bonded, the Shadow would get his immortality, and he could share some of her powers if they were compatible with his.

Both men looked as if someone had smacked them upside the head with a bat. Brody recovered first.

"Well shit. Dennis is a dead wolf walking then."

# Chapter Four

Sheila plopped down into a booth, exhausted. It had been a long night. After she had helped Mr. Dionne with going over his insurance paperwork for his business, she worked on the third floor of the club. It had been unusually busy for a Thursday night.

Probably because word had gone out over the Supernatural grapevine that the Master of the City was present. People had flocked to the club to see if they could spot the elusive Nightshade.

Living in Las Vegas, Sheila had been exposed to Nightshade growing up. After all, it was the seat of the North American Nightshade Queen. So, a master of a city wasn't a novelty for her. Not when the council members regularly came to town.

She reached into her bodice and pulled out some bills. Most of her tips were with the floor manager. She allowed the waitresses to drop them with her, so they didn't have to worry about losing them. She had nearly one hundred in her hand and another three or four hundred in the back office.

Just her tips alone would allow her to save for a nice place at the end of her probation period. She could also restore part of her go-bag cash, which was a top priority for her. She would not lose her hard-won knowledge or experience to being comfortable. Just because she hadn't heard anything about Dennis in the area, that didn't mean she wouldn't need to flee at a moment's notice. Hopefully, he gave up on finding her.

Lena flopped down on the opposite side of the booth. "Did you see the Master of the City?"

"Nope. The only Nightshade that I spotted was the one I bumped into on the elevator earlier."

And that was enough for her. Her body remembered their brief touch. Sheila flushed at the memory of her reaction. One would have thought that he caressed her private parts with fingers instead of the brief bump between the two of them. He was someone she wouldn't mind bumping into in a dark bedroom. Preferably with no clothes between them.

The bartender gave her a look filled with disbelief. "I can't believe you. That was Xavier! The others were right when they said you were clueless."

Sheila's mouth dropped open in surprise. Then, she felt her face flush. "I ran into the Master of Cleveland. Oh, shit."

"Well, you must have made an impression on him." Lena's eyes danced with mirth. "Rumor on the floor has it he watched you like a hawk until you came down here for your shift."

What she wouldn't admit to her friend was that she felt him looking at her from time to time. But since the Alpha and the other Nightshade at the table were looking at her, she read nothing into it. She really would not mention that she could still feel where he had touched her.

Sheila fanned herself, trying to cool down. "Is all the cleanup done?" She really wanted to go back to her apartment and pass out.

"I believe so." Lena gave her friend a wide smile. "Now about the Master..."

Before Sheila could respond, Mari, the club manager, came up to their table. The tall Hispanic woman was a member of the local lion pride. The gossip among the staff was that she and Brody were an item. But no one could prove it.

Both Sheila and Lena stared at the manager, who was unusually grim faced.

"You're going to have to wait a lot longer to go home." Her voice was flat.

Sheila's heart sank. She just wanted to go home and sleep. "Why?"

"Tonight, one woman of the Pack was attacked, and the attacker also hurt a Nightshade." Mia's eyes paused on both women, but to Sheila, it seemed as if her gaze lingered longer on her.

"That's why Brody was in such a foul mood tonight," remarked Lena to herself.

"All of you will get rides back to your homes by the Enforcers."

That would not work. She had driven herself and two of the other waitresses who lived in her building to work.

"My truck!" Ever since someone in the Pack had taken care of all the legalities of her ownership of the truck, she loved it. The last thing she wanted to do was leave it downtown.

"An Enforcer will drive it back for you." Mia's tone left no room for discussion.

"When can we leave?" asked Lena.

"You're riding with the Alpha."

"Of course. I'll probably have to stay tonight at the house with him." She rolled her eyes.

Since Lena was Brody's only niece, he would protect her. He had raised her since she was ten. Lena's parents had been killed during an attempted coup of their home Pack. He had given up his bachelor life to raise her.

Sheila resigned herself to a long wait to go home. "Who am I going with?"

Mia looked relieved that they didn't argue with her. Some of the other waitresses probably gave her grief about waiting to go home. "Eric. He's already on a run, so you'll head out once he returns."

"What about tomorrow? Are we allowed to come in as normal?" asked Lena.

"You'll get a call from the packhouse letting you know what to do tomorrow."

The farther that Xavier's SUV moved from the hotel, the more uneasy he felt. This wasn't like him at all. He mostly dealt in probabilities, not in the mystical side of his vampire nature.

He leaned forward. "Turn around and head back for the club." His driver wisely said nothing. But the other guard riding shotgun turned around.

"Sir, is something wrong?"

"I think so." Xavier closed his eyes and pushed his senses out. As a Master of the City, he had the power to sense trouble in his area of influence. That was when he used the power.

There was some sort of malevolent presence nearby, and Xavier was afraid that he knew exactly who the presence was targeting.

There was no way that he would allow Sheila to be harmed. While he wouldn't be killed if she died, he would be severely hurt. And that would allow others to try to take over his territory by challenging him.

Whoever it was targeting Sheila would discover what a very pissed off Nightshade could do in protecting his Shadow. He would show no mercy. Not a bit.

# Chapter Five

Someone was targeting his Shadow—the lone wolf, who did not know that she belonged to him. His eyes opened, and they were glowing a deep yellow.

"Someone is after my Shadow." His instincts were screaming for him to protect Sheila.

To his credit, his guard quickly reacted. He pulled out his cell phone and quickly dialed a number. "Is anyone close to The Howling Wolf?" He paused. "Get them there, stat. Protect the women coming out. One of them is the Master's Shadow."

Xavier pulled out his phone and opened the text app. *Damien, where are you?*

*Leaving The Howling Wolf.*

*Watch Sheila until I get there. I think there might be another attack.*

*Gotcha!*

Xavier hoped his preparations were enough. He shouldn't have left the club without her. Silly him, that he thought he could take his time getting to know her. His phone dinged. *She's left already. We're going to catch up with them.*

Five minutes later, Xavier opened the truck door. He was about to speak when he heard a scream, and then growling and snarling.

*Fuck!* Xavier took off, running at top speed toward the sounds. If any normal humans had been around, they would have thought that he vanished, he moved so fast. Less than thirty seconds later and two blocks over, he found the source of the trouble.

Three men and two wolves surrounded Sheila, another woman, and a man. The woman looked frightened and was just shaking. However, his Shadow looked pissed. She had kicked off her heels and looked as if she could chew nails.

"Watch it, bitch. Our orders are to take you back. We can hurt you and still follow orders." The speaker was a massive man whose nose looked as if someone had broken it many times over his life.

Sheila growled, "Touch me and lose a paw." Her eyes had changed to that of her wolf's.

Good—his Shadow wasn't a wilting flower. If she could back up her threat, she wouldn't have any issues in his Court.

Xavier felt his guards run up behind him, and he cleared his throat loudly. All the eyes in the alley turned his way. "How dare you enter my city and attack those under my protection?"

The one who had been threatening Sheila turned to him. "I don't know who you are, but this is none of your business."

Oh, this thug wasn't the brightest bulb in the shed. Xavier threw his hand out, sending out telekinetic power that slammed the man dead in the chest. The force of the power slammed him a few feet back into a wall. A wet, meaty crack sounded. Something in that fool had broken. He didn't move again.

"I am Xavier Silversbane, Master of Cleveland." He stepped closer, and the attackers eyed him warily. "Who sent you?"

One wolf growled at him, then yelped as he too went flying into a wall before landing unconscious. *Damn!* He couldn't pull that trick too many more times without being laid out from the power drain. But the odds were now in their favor, with only three of the attackers still standing.

He could tell the wolf was still alive but unconscious. Good, they could question him later.

His guards and the wolf with Sheila had moved, so that they covered the other jerks in the alley.

Movement caught his eye at the other end of the alley. He looked at the remaining three. "You really don't want me to repeat myself."

One man glanced at Sheila before returning his attention to Xavier. "She's a wanted criminal back in Las Vegas. We're to bring her back for a Pack trial."

Xavier shook his head. The idiot's lie was so obvious, it was painful. "Wrong answer." His eyes glowed yellow in the darkness. He felt his fangs descend. "Kill them."

A scream of pain erupted from the thug that had spoken before fading to a gurgle. Damien's knife had erupted from his chest to stick out the other side. The fool hadn't heard the Nightshade ghost up behind him.

The death of the thug threw off the focus of the rest of the group. His guards, along with the two Nightshade that had followed Damien into the alleyway, made quick work of them.

After making sure that the unconscious wolf, who had shifted back to human form, was tied up for questioning, Xavier made his way over to Sheila.

She and the other woman had moved to the side of the alley. She had her arm around the other woman and was attempting to calm her down.

Xavier was glad to see that his Shadow was made of stern stuff. She would need that in order to survive in his Court. "Are you two alright?" He pitched his voice to only reach their ears.

"Yes, just a little shaken." Sheila looked up at her before hugging the woman beside her. "It's ok. You're safe now."

He really didn't feel like dealing with a crying she-wolf. Glancing around, he spotted the guard who had been with the pair. He motioned for him to come over.

A minute later, he and Sheila stood alone. While everyone else stood only a few feet away, it felt to him they were alone in their own little world.

"We were never properly introduced." Xavier grabbed her hand and brought it up to his lips. He kissed it and fought down a satisfied smile at the perplexed expression on her face. "My name is Xavier Silversbane."

"Uh…" Her hand shook slightly in his. "I'm Sheila Carter." She tugged slightly, but Xavier pretended not to notice.

It wasn't part of his plan to allow her to gather herself together. He wanted her to come with him back to the Tower.

There was no way that he was allowing her to go back to her apartment. The asshole that was after her would not have another chance at her.

He dropped her hand and stepped up close. It forced Sheila to look up at his face. She was clearly flustered but did not step back.

"While I wish it wasn't under these circumstances, I'm happy to have found you."

"Found me?" His Shadow's face turned suspicious.

Flashes of distrust hit Xavier like a truck, along with a healthy dose of fear. Their fledgling Bond had decided on a bad time to come to life.

"Yes." Xavier put all the warmth he had into his voice. The fear and suspicion had him tossing his tentative plans into the garbage. "You're my Shadow."

# Chapter Six

*His what?* Sheila couldn't have heard the words correctly. "Your Shadow?" This had to be a bad dream. First, she had been nearly kidnapped by Dennis's goons, and now some vampire was telling her she was his Shadow? His freaking life mate!

Scratch that. Not some vampire, but the Master of the City? This had to be a dream... or nightmare depending on how she looked at it. There was no way that she was the soul mate to a vampire. Her wolf disagreed, whining and trying to get her to rub against him.

He nodded. "I had planned on meeting you another night and talking to you."

She swallowed and tried to take a step back. He prevented it by grabbing her shoulders. The shock of his touch sent a shiver down her spine. "How did you know I was in trouble?"

"I could feel something out of place. So, I came back to the bar, then I heard the fight."

"Oh. How do you know that I'm your Shadow?" she asked, trying to stall for enough time to think.

"Every Nightshade can identify their Shadow at first sight." Xavier ran his hand up and down her forearm slowly, and tingles erupted through her body in response. "I knew you were mine when you stepped into the elevator earlier." His eyes slowly faded from the angry yellow of earlier to a dark color. It was hard in the dim light of the alley to make out their actual shade.

She didn't know what to say to that. Sheila was still freaked out by everything that had happened in the past twenty minutes. So, she did what she normally did around cute men. She froze like a rabbit.

The Nightshade bent and placed a gentle kiss on her lips. Of course, her wolf picked this time to make an appearance. It started yipping in excitement. The blasted thing wanted Sheila to jump the vampire's bones right there in the alley.

It was all that Sheila could do to prevent her wolf from taking her over and humping him right there in the street. She would not reflect on the shivery sensation that his lips caused her when he kissed her. Nope, not at all.

"Come on, I'll take you home." Xavier took her hand and started walking to where four Nightshade and the wolf from Brody's pack stood talking.

"I want to get Sheila out of here. Damien, clean up here and let Brody know I'm taking care of Sheila."

A tall, light-haired man, who must have been Damien, nodded. "I got this."

Xavier didn't say another word. He started out of the alley, towing Sheila with him. Two of the Nightshade peeled off to follow them. By the time they were on the street, one guard was in front while the other one followed the pair.

Normally, Sheila would have a problem with Xavier's high-handedness, but there had been too many shocks that evening for her to process.

Dennis had tracked her down. She shouldn't have let her guard down. But the Cleveland Pack had done so much for her over the past month. They welcomed her with open arms and made it clear she was one of theirs.

Now, Pack members were being attacked just because they took her in.

How in the hell did Dennis find her? Sheila was sure that she left no tracks behind. She was careful not to leave electronic tracks for anyone to find her.

A few minutes later, Xavier was handing her into the back of an armored Escalade. He sat beside her as the two guards got into the front.

She turned to him. "Thanks for the ride. You can drop me off at the Pack apartments."

"You're heading to the Tower tonight." Xavier looked over at her as he made his statement.

No way was she going to the Tower.

To humans, it was a larger, mixed commercial and residential hi-rise in downtown Cleveland. In reality, it was the seat of the Nightshade Court.

Supernatural businesses filled the commercial part of the building. The residential part was mostly Nightshade and support staff of the Nightshade Court.

"No. I'd like to go home." Sheila wanted to be in her own space, so she could think without Xavier's distracting presence.

"That's not going to happen." The flatness in Xavier's tone surprised her. "You've already been attacked once this evening. What makes you think they won't come for you when you're at your apartment?"

Sheila's mouth froze on her next retort. Did Dennis's goons know where she lived? If they didn't, it would only be a matter of time before they found her apartment.

"Oh, gods. I have to get out of town!" Her voice rose until it was high-pitched. She started shaking.

Faster than sight, Xavier reached out and pulled her into his chest. She shook violently as her face pressed against his shirt.

"You don't have to flee," said Xavier quietly as he rubbed her back. "You'll be safe with me."

"Dennis killed my family. Now, he's after me." Sheila tried to calm down, but her world was imploding around her. Her wolf paced in agitation inside of her.

Xavier's arms tightened around her. Then released her. When she sat back, he looked deep into her teary eyes. "Dennis won't touch you. I'll kill him before he lays a finger on you."

What she saw in his eyes should have chilled her to the bone. Staring at her was the Master of the City, a Nightshade who knew his own power and wore it like a familiar set of clothes.

Instead, something in her relaxed. It might be safe to believe him. Her shaking stopped, and her breathing slowed down to normal. "Okay."

"Good. We'll talk more tomorrow about this so-called Alpha." He took her hand. "Tonight, we'll get you settled into the Tower."

Sheila didn't know that his definition of getting her settled meant her staying in his penthouse.

The Silver Tower was a modern skyscraper in the Cleveland skyline. Xavier's predecessor had built it. At the time of its creation, it was the tallest building in Cleveland. Now, it was the second largest after the construction of the Terminal Tower.

Xavier had the building redone and the facade changed shortly after the start of his reign. His predecessor had grandiose notions about his place in the world. And the Tower had reflected it.

Sheila tried not to gawk as they pulled up to the Tower. Instead of pulling up at the valet entrance as she expected, they drove into an underground parking garage.

"Why didn't we use the valet parking?"

The driver answered. "Paparazzi, ma 'am. Master Xavier is a celebrity in Cleveland."

"Oh. I'm sorry I didn't catch your names earlier."

"I'm Tim, and my partner is Robert." The other guard turned and bobbed his head politely before turning to scan outside of the truck.

The light from the garage showed Xavier's grimace clearly. "For some reason, the humans want to follow my life."

Sheila could think of a few reasons without even trying—his looks, money, and that he was a recluse. Hell, most of the Supernaturals that came to The Howling Wolf gossiped about him. Most thought he had some secret swinger lifestyle. Oh, how they would be so disappointed to find out he was just a private person.

"I bet it's part of life as the Master of the City."

The SUV pulled into a spot marked "Reserved" that was near an elevator. There were no other spaces for at least twenty feet in any direction.

Xavier got out and then helped Sheila out of the truck. "You'll be able to tell me soon enough."

"Why?" Sheila tried to take her hand back, but the infuriating Nightshade refused to let it go.

He gave her a small smile. "As my Shadow, you'll be in the spotlight as well." He chuckled at the dumbfounded look on her face.

The small group entered the elevator. Tim inserted a key card before punching a button for the 30th floor.

Upon exiting on the 30th floor, Xavier explained they had to go to another elevator across the building to get to the top five floors, where his Court lived, for security reasons.

Even at the late hour of four A.M., there were plenty of people about the 30th floor. From what Sheila could make out during the quick walk, his business occupied this floor. Most of those in the hallway were Nightshade.

Everyone in the hallway greeted Xavier with respect and stared at Sheila with open curiosity. A few of the looks were slightly hostile.

*Great.* She knew she was going to be gossiped about for the rest of the night.

They arrived at another elevator, and Tim inserted his card on the outside to open the doors.

"Only those who live in the residences have access to this elevator," said Tim as the doors opened.

"Make sure that security inputs Sheila in tomorrow."

Tim nodded. "Yes, sir. I'll leave a message with the day shift."

It took some willpower for Sheila not to react to Xavier's assumption that she would remain at the Tower. She would just lie low for a few days and then take off for another city. Or better yet, leave the United States. There had to be somewhere in the world that was safe from Dennis.

The elevator doors opened up into a modern foyer. Light travertine marble covered the floors. And off to the side of the elevator was a chair for the comfort of whom was waiting for the elevator. To the other side was a door that clearly led to the stairwell. The foyer opened out to a long room that had floor-to-ceiling windows. The view out those windows would be breathtaking, no matter the season.

Xavier turned to his guards. "You two relax. I'm not leaving the penthouse until I go into the office tomorrow."

After the two left, Xavier walked into the kitchen with Sheila trailing after him. "Would you like something to drink?"

"I'm good. Where am I staying tonight?" It was time to cut to the chase with him. She was exhausted and wanted to sleep. She was not in the mood for the games that her body was demanding they get into. Hopefully, when she woke up, she would find out this was just a bad dream.

Reaching into a cabinet, he took down a glass. "Here, of course."

"No. Seriously, I can't stay here." Sheila went to the opposite side of the kitchen to glare at him.

He raised an eyebrow. "I don't see why not. You are my Shadow, after all."

She held up a finger. "First, we don't know each other." Then, she held up a second finger. "Second, I will be leaving."

"Stop." Xavier's voice held a touch of command. Sheila put her hand down and glared at him.

He set the glass down on the white marble countertop and prowled over to her. Xavier purposely crowded her space, staring intently down at her with sexy, brown eyes. "There is no way in the hell I'll let you go with that crazy ass Alpha after you."

Sheila's mouth dropped open at the sheer audacity of this man. *Who in the hell did he think he was?*

"Second," his voice deepened into a throaty purr, "you're mine."

Before Sheila could form a response, Xavier bent his head down to kiss her.

A sharp spark of power raced through Sheila as Xavier's lips covered hers. Although she wanted to remain unmoving, she responded to his kiss.

Her wolf started prancing around inside of her like a lovesick puppy.

She felt his arms slide around her waist as he kissed her witless. After a few more seconds, he lifted his head.

"Don't think a kiss will solve this issue." Instead of the warning she wanted her voice to have, it came out nearly breathless.

Xavier's answering smile was full of sensual promise. "Of course not."

Before Sheila could say anything else, Xavier picked her up and headed deeper into the penthouse.

"What are you doing?" Sheila could feel his chest rumble with a chuckle.

"Moving our discussion to some place more comfortable."

Xavier carried her down a hallway that led to one of the largest bedrooms that she had ever been in.

Sheila's attention was drawn to the floor-to-ceiling windows in the bedroom. Someone had opened the blinds to reveal the city skyline. It was a breathtaking view.

"Your place has magnificent views." She knew she was babbling. The effortless way that Xavier carried her was getting to her.

Xavier stopped beside a massive bed covered with a black, silk quilt. "Not as good of a view as what I have." He dropped her on the bed.

She gave a small cry as she bounced on the mattress. Before she could do more than sit up, Xavier had removed his shirt. He was standing there, looking scrumptious in just his dress slacks.

Her wolf howled in her mind. Sheila hissed for it to hush mentally, but the silly beast was happy at seeing Xavier partially naked. Well, to be honest, she was happy to see his ripped chest as well. *What did this man lift to look this good?*

"As much as I love seeing you in that little black number, I think you would look much better out of it." Xavier held up his right hand, and his nails grew to about three inches.

He wasn't going to rip her... And with a lightning-fast move, Xavier had used his nails to rip her dress right down the middle. He had only sliced the dress and not her skin or underwear.

Sheila didn't know if she should be scared or impressed at his level of control. She looked down at her ruined dress and went with impressed for her sanity. "Really? It would have taken me a couple of seconds to take it off."

A slow smile spread on Xavier's face. "It was more fun this way." He undid his pants and stepped out of them before getting on the bed. He wasn't wearing any underwear at all.

She couldn't help but look at his rod as he climbed up beside her. It was large and demanding her attention. She grew wet as she imagined how he would stretch her.

Xavier took a deep breath. "You smell so sweet." He leaned over and gave her a kiss before pulling back to stare at her. Sheila shivered under his intense gaze. Goosebumps formed along her skin.

"There are so many things that I want to do to you." Xavier's voice was a deep, raspy growl. He hooked one finger over the waist band of her panties and pulled it down and off her.

His voice alone caused her to grow damp. "Then what's stopping you?" she asked.

Sheila would have clapped her hands over her mouth if they weren't busy exploring Xavier's body. She couldn't believe that she actually said that out loud. *Me and my big mouth.*

Xavier's answering grin could have lit up the Cleveland skyline. "Nothing."

With that, he started kissing his way down her body. He gave each breast attention with his tongue before he moved down to her belly. She nearly jumped out of her skin when his tongue delved into her belly button. Who knew that she was ticklish there?

A dark chuckle was Sheila's only warning before Xavier settled between her legs. "What do we have here?"

Sheila tried to prop herself up on her elbows so she could see him. To her surprise, his eyes were glowing yellow. She shivered.

His fingers spread apart her folds. "I see you're wet for me already." He bent his head and gave her an intimate kiss.

Electricity shot up from his lips through her core and up to the rest of her body. Sheila started panting when he pulled back and slid a finger inside of her. "Do you want more?"

Sheila nodded.

"Out loud, my dear, or I stop." His hand didn't move.

When this was over, she'd kill him for certain. You did not tease a she-wolf like this and get away with it. "Yes!"

Xavier didn't say another word. He resumed his kiss while working his finger inside her. A minute later, he added a second finger to his administration.

Sheila wanted more than what he was giving her, although it did feel amazing. She wanted his shaft inside of her more than anything in the world. She gripped his shoulders and pulled him up.

Xavier took the hint and settled his thighs between hers. His eyes locked with hers. "You belong to me." Before Sheila could respond to that possessive statement, he surged into her.

He was definitely larger than he appeared. Sheila wrapped her legs around his waist and pulled him closer. While she wasn't a virgin by a long shot, it had been a while since her last partner. She felt herself stretching out around him.

"So, what are you waiting on?" she taunted. "The next coming?"

"I'll show you the next coming." Xavier started moving within her. Sheila could do nothing more than hold onto him as he took her on a magical ride.

# Chapter Seven

Sheila slid out of bed as if she was just heading to the bathroom. She knew from hard-earned lessons in her youth that if you tried to sneak around, someone would notice. But if you acted normal, most sleeping people wouldn't move a muscle.

It was just before dawn, and Xavier was passed out cold. Between the fight outside and their lovemaking a short while ago, he had expended a lot of energy. She just hoped that it was enough to keep him sleeping.

Instead of going into the bathroom, Sheila padded out into the hallway and quietly closed the door. She paused, listening for sounds of Xavier waking up. There was nothing. Good.

She looked down at herself. Crap, she needed clothing. She stopped outside of another bedroom. Maybe there would be clothing she could borrow. Hell, she could wear one of Xavier's shirts and act like it was a dress. All she needed was to get down to street level.

There, she would change into a wolf and run for her apartment. With any luck, she could be on the road out of Cleveland in a few hours.

"Where do you think you're going?"

"Fuck!" Sheila screeched as she jumped into the air. She whirled around to face a nude Xavier, who was standing behind her. "Don't creep up behind me."

"Were you thinking about leaving?" Xavier's eyes glowed yellow in the dim light of the hallway. He didn't seem all that happy to her.

She put her hand over her rapidly beating heart and tried to will herself to calm down. He couldn't prove she was leaving. "That wasn't nice scaring me like that."

Xavier stepped forward, crowding her against the wall. He put his hands on either side of her head and leaned forward. His fangs descended, and his eyes glowed brighter. "You wouldn't have gotten past the 30th floor before someone caught you and brought you back to me."

He was too far into her personal space. Sheila's fright was slowly morphing into anger. How dare he keep her trapped in the Tower? "You have no right to keep me here. I need to get out of town fast."

"If you had gotten out of the Tower, Dennis's men would have caught you before you got outside of city limits." Xavier's voice was a low growl. "By now, I'm sure he has your apartment staked out."

If she had gone home last night, she probably would have made it out before Dennis found out where she lived. Her time at the Tower gave his men more time to find her.

"Then help me get out of town. I can flee the States. I have family over in Britain that might help me." Sheila pushed at Xavier's chest, but he didn't budge.

"No." Xavier leaned closer so that his face was inches away from hers. "You're my Shadow. I'll protect you. Right now, my people are trying to find Dennis." His lips touched hers briefly. "You're safe here."

How in the hell could she get Xavier to understand that she had to leave? People were getting harassed and bullied just because they knew her. It would solve a lot of problems if she could just leave.

"I'm not worth all the trouble," she whispered.

Xavier's expression softened. His eyes faded from their angry yellow back to their normal, dark color. His hands slid down the wall until they were even with her waist before coming to rest on it.

"I spoke with Brody about you today. Both he and his pack are impressed with you." His arms slid around her waist. "And I think you're selling yourself short."

Sheila opened her mouth to speak, but Xavier stopped her words with a light kiss.

"I don't know what you went through before you got here. But you, Sheila Davis, are someone worthy of help. And there are people lined up to give you that help."

"But..."

"Sshh... But nothing." Xavier touched his forehead to hers. "I want you to promise me something."

"What?" Sheila couldn't keep the suspicion out of her voice. She learned early on in life to never give a promise without hearing the entire request. That was the fastest way to get oneself into a lot of trouble.

"Give me a week to find Dennis before you run. You'll be safe here at the Tower."

Sheila nodded.

"No. I want to hear the words." Xavier pulled back and stared down at her.

*Damn.* That trick normally worked on others.

"I promise to give you a week before I leave." She could use that time to find a place to run to. And to find someone who could get her a passport under another name. Hopefully, she had enough money hidden away to spring for it.

"Thank you. Now let's head back to bed. I'm tired."

# Chapter Eight

S omething warm and silky enveloped Sheila. Her senses told her she was lying in the softest of sheets. She tried to open her eyes, and she thought she heard a whispered, "Sleep, baby." She fell back asleep.

Hours later, Sheila opened her eyes. The room was completely dark. The bed that she was in felt strange. This wasn't her bed. Then, memories of the night before slammed into her like a freight train. She shivered as she played back their lovemaking and her escape attempt.

*What was I thinking?*

Sheila groaned. She never slept with men she had just met. In fact, she'd only ever had two partners in her life.

Thank the Moon Goddess that she was alone. Waking up next to Xavier might have been too much.

She rolled over to see a clock glowing on the nightstand. It was 6 P.M. She'd slept the day away.

"I need a shower." Sheila groped at the lamp on the nightstand. Once she turned on the light, she saw a note.

*I'll be back up to meet you around 8 P.M. There's food in the kitchen. My assistant left some clothes for you on the couch. Don't leave the penthouse without a guard. Xavier.*

Sheila rolled her eyes at the autocratic message. Muttering about over-bearing males, she got up and went for a shower.

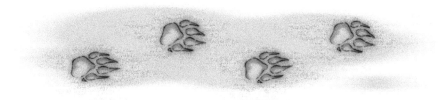

Xavier was standing in front of the treated windows, looking out over the Cleveland skyline, when Damien entered. He didn't bother to turn around. "So, that Alpha Dennis is behind the attacks?"

He heard Damien put something down on the desk. "Yes. The captive says that he sent them to catch Sheila."

Xavier toned away from the window. "That doesn't explain why they are attacking members of my Court."

His second held up a finger. "They were here to cause trouble for Brody."

That brought Xavier pause. Who would try to stir up shit for the Cleveland Pack? While Wolf Pack politics was an actual issue, this was outside of the norms.

There wasn't enough information to solve this riddle. There was no logical reason for a Pack from the Southwest to be messing with a Pack from the Midwest.

"Did he say if his Alpha was in town?"

Damien shook his head. "He tried lying, but eventually, he caved. He didn't know if his Alpha was here. Apparently, when there is an operation this large, several groups are sent out. And each group doesn't know about the next."

"And of course, the one I took out was probably the one with the info." Next time, he would think before just killing. Maybe. Well, if Sheila wasn't involved.

All bets were off the table if it involved his Shadow.

"You left one alive." Damon picked up his phone from Xavier's desk. He tapped at it. "I've got people tracing the steps they took to find them."

Xavier returned to his desk and sat down. He pulled up a file that he had gotten shortly after he woke. He sent it to Damien's folder on the server. They almost never sent emails about his territory's business.

"The investigator found that the deaths of Sheila's family were ruled as a murder-suicide."

"What? An entire family was slaughtered! Who would believe that?" Damien's face was almost comical in its disbelief.

Xavier knew that his own face was probably grim. "A sheriff who isn't too interested in a family of known criminals. Or who was paid to look the other way?"

It was just as well that the humans weren't too interested in looking into the murders, even though that bothered him more than he cared to admit. The human police might think that Sheila was the one who killed them. Or worse, find out that the family wasn't human. The last thing the Supernatural community needed was the human authorities finding out about them.

Xavier hadn't been alive the last time some nosy humans had nearly outed the Supernatural community. The residents of a small town had found out about a local Lion Pride and the Magician that had mated into the Pride.

The town had been in a valley. One night, a rockslide unexpectedly came down the side of the mountain, burying the town and all its residents.

Only the few humans that had close friends or had mated into the Pride survived.

"Her brother that survived is missing." Damien swiped at his phone. "If he was smart, he took off after warning Sheila."

If he wanted to be honest with himself, Xavier didn't care if the brother survived. It was the actions of her family that got Sheila into this mess. Everything that he learned about the brother suggested that he was no good.

"Keep an eye out. I don't want her brother showing up here at the Tower." Xavier frowned at his second. "I have a feeling if he finds out Sheila is my Shadow, he will appear."

Before Damien could answer, there was a knock at the door. He recognized her distinctive knock. "Come in, Anita."

The pretty brunette assistant walked in, holding her tablet. "Good evening, sir, Damien. You wanted me to remind you about the Lionne fundraiser tomorrow?"

Fuck, he had totally forgotten about the event. The Lionne fundraiser was an annual end-of-summer gala that raised money for the Lionne Foundation.

The local Pride ran the Lionne Foundation and focused on helping children in need. While the public front of the foundation helped human children, the primary focus was to help Supernatural children.

He could not skip the event. Which meant that Sheila would be introduced as his Shadow sooner than he thought.

"Anita, my Shadow is going to need an outfit for the gala."

His assistant went slightly pale. "Your Shadow?"

"Yes. Yesterday, I found my Shadow." Xavier went back to his laptop and began typing. "You'll meet her later. Tim's getting her built into the Tower systems today."

"I understand. Did you need anything else, sir?" Anita started backing toward the door. When Xavier shook his head without looking up, she left the room.

Damien watched her depart with a slight frown. He made a mental note to speak to the woman later.

# Chapter Nine

Xavier stared in awe at the scene he was greeted with in the kitchen. His Shadow's luscious ass was in a lacy pair of panties. She was bent over in front of the open fridge. From the sounds coming from inside, she was looking for something to eat.

He leaned against the wall, enjoying the view until she stood up. Her hands were filled with a box of what smelled like fried chicken. She smiled at him.

"I hope you weren't trying to scare me. I heard and smelled you." She set the box on the counter.

Xavier gave her a leisurely look from her head to pink-painted toes. She only wore a t-shirt and panties. From the aromatic scent of her body wash, she hadn't been out of the shower long.

She pointed at her eyes. "My face is up here."

"Yes, it is." Xavier walked over to her and took her hand in his. He raised it up to his lips and kissed the inside of her wrist. "But since you are dressed so nicely, I had to look."

Sheila chuckled nervously. "Oh no, we're not heading back to your bedroom!"

A very untrustworthy grin crossed his lips as he scented her arousal. "Who says we need a bedroom?" He let go of her hand and wrapped his large hands around her waist to lift her onto the counter.

She was now eye-level with him. Shock was clear in her brown eyes. He leaned in and kissed her. The minty flavor of her toothpaste mixed with her natural flavor exploded on his lips.

"There are so many things I can do to you that don't involve a bed," he whispered against her lips.

"Like what?" Sheila's voice held a dare.

"Something like this." Xavier spread her legs and stepped inside them. Then, he used a finger to push aside the center of her panties to trail a finger down her folds.

"Oh..." Sheila sighed. She clutched at his arms while his fingers explored her lower regions.

He quickly drenched his finger, and using her slickness, he slid it inside of her. Sheila gasped in surprise and arched her back. Chuckling, he added a second finger to join the first.

Xavier's eyes glowed with desire as he played with his Shadow. Her emotions were clear through their growing Bond. It wouldn't take much to bring her to orgasm. Hell, his arousal was so powerful that it would only take a small breeze to set him off.

A chime sounded from the entry. Xavier swore. Someone had just keyed the elevator for the penthouse.

"What?" Sheila asked, sitting up straight.

"Someone is on their way up." He jumped back in surprise when Sheila suddenly shrieked. She hopped off the counter and ran for the bedroom.

Stifling a groan, he went over to the sink to wash his hands. Not that whoever was heading up wouldn't be able to smell what he'd been doing with Sheila.

A minute later, the elevator door opened to admit Tim and Anita. His assistant had several shopping bags in her hands.

Anita noticed Xavier looking at the bags in her hands. "I had a personal shopper pick up a few outfits for Sheila to get her by until she can shop for her own stuff."

Xavier nodded. Until they resolved the issues with the rogue Alpha, circumstances would limit Sheila in where she could go.

Tim held what looked to be a laptop bag. "I have her keycard, a phone, and a laptop for Miss Sheila."

The three went into the living room. Sheila joined them a minute later, dressed in her same t-shirt, but this time with leggings.

Anita smiled at Sheila brightly. "Hello, I'm Anita, Xavier's assistant."

"I'm Sheila. Do I have you to thank for the clothes this afternoon?" Sheila walked over and shook Anita's hand.

"Sorry for limited options. I had to guess at your size." Anita motioned to the bags on the table. "I brought you some more clothes."

"Hiya, Tim." Sheila nodded at the guard.

Tim blushed and bobbed his head at her. "I brought you a new phone and laptop."

"You didn't have to go to the trouble. I have a phone already," said Sheila. "It's in the bedroom."

Xavier patted the seat on the couch beside him. Sheila gave him a sharp look but sat beside him. Her expression warned him to behave.

He would behave, but only because his employees did not need to see him ravish his Shadow. There would be enough rumors about the two of them without him adding more. Yet.

"Sheila, now that you're associated with the Tower, your electronics will be issued by the Court." He shook his head when she opened her mouth to protest. "Like it or not, you're a part of my Court and that of my Liege, Lord Andre."

"What about my Pack? I was to be admitted this fall." Xavier could tell that the full realization of what it meant for her to be his Shadow had just hit her.

He sighed. "Per the treaties between the shifters and Nightshade, my claim supersedes your Pack's claim."

Sheila closed her eyes and pinched the bridge of her nose. The struggle she was having to contain her emotions was potent through their Bond.

"Can I transfer my contacts to my new phone?" The emotion flowing to him via their link clearly told him that this conversation wasn't over. She was just putting it aside for later. Which was fine with him since it didn't need to be held with an audience.

"If you give me the phone, our IT team will move your data over after they check your phone," said Tim. "We have to make sure nothing is transferred into our network."

"Fine, but I need to write a couple of numbers that I need to call tonight."

"Brody's aware that you aren't coming in tonight."

Sheila paused, her eyes flashing with irritation. The restraint she used to not snap at him was clear. She took a deep breath. "I still need to let the ladies that ride with me know they have to find another ride tonight." She turned and left the living room.

There was an awkward silence in the room until Anita broke it by bringing up some administrative details that they needed to review. The three discussed matters pertaining to his businesses until Sheila returned a few minutes later

Sheila sat back down beside Xavier. "Brody passes his greetings and says he'll see you tomorrow night."

Anita turned slightly, so that she was facing Sheila. "In a little while, staff from a boutique here in the Tower will be up with some outfits for the Lionne Gala."

"The what?" asked Sheila with some confusion.

"The Lionne Gala. You and I have to attend it tomorrow." Xavier eyed his Shadow, but she didn't react like he thought, although she shot him a narrow-eyed glance. He imagined that she would have plenty to say once they were alone.

"Is this a Supernatural or human event?" She leaned back on the couch and crossed her legs.

For a brief second, Xavier imagined her legs wrapped around his waist as he rode her. He had to wrench his mind away from that erotic image and force himself to pay attention to the conversation.

"It's an annual event thrown by the local Lion Pride," said Tim. "It raises money to fund the Lionne Foundation."

Anita took up the explanation. "The Lionne Foundation helps Supernatural children with education, housing, and other needs if the parents can't help."

They discussed the details of the gala until Anita's phone pinged. "The boutique owner and her staff are on their way up here for the dress selection."

That sounded like torture to Xavier. "I'll head back to work." He leaned over and gave Sheila a kiss on the cheek.

# Chapter Ten

The last three hours passed in a blur as Sheila tried on several outfits that the shop owner, a Nightshade named Penny, had brought for her to try on.

She hadn't been happy with any of the dresses brought up. They were all boring. None were ugly, but they reminded Sheila of something that a Stepford wife would wear.

"Do you have a particular style that you're looking for?" asked Penny after the fifth dress.

Sheila tried not to show the relief she felt at the woman's question. She actually liked the tall, statuesque shop owner and didn't want to hurt her feelings. "I've spent most of my life trying to blend in so that no one noticed me." She paused, trying to think of the right words. "I want something that will cause people to look."

Penny's answering smile was so bright that anyone could have seen it on the other side of the city. "You want to make an impression?"

"Yes. It is my first outing here in Cleveland as a Supernatural." If this event was as special as she thought it was, the Supernatural world would be out in full force. If she was going to be on Xavier's arm, then she was going to shine. She was tired of always fading into the background, trying not to be noticed.

She could hear her father's voice in her mind. "Baby girl, sometimes the best disguise is to be so outrageous that everyone misses the real you." Of course, he meant that regarding pulling a con. But it still worked for other aspects of life. Like hiding in plain sight from a crazy ass Alpha.

The shopkeeper turned to one of her assistants. "Go get the green gown and my box." As the assistant turned to leave, she added, "Call Alonzo and tell him we'll need to borrow some jewelry for the event."

Anita, who had been scrolling through her phone, looked up. "Remember, she'll be representing the Court."

The assistant had been pushing for Sheila to choose the most boring of the dresses. She'd been downright pushy about it.

Too bad for Anita that Sheila was stubborn as a mule. If Sheila's family couldn't bully her into a life of crime, no human was going to choose what clothing she wore.

Penny just ignored Anita. "While we wait for the gown, look through my website and see if there is anything else I can get you."

The second assistant brought over a tablet and handed it to Sheila. Penny and Sheila discussed the merits of different outfits while they waited on the first assistant to return to the penthouse. They both pretended not to hear Anita muttering about representing the Court.

By the time the assistant returned with a dress bag and a second tote filled with accessories, Sheila had chosen three more outfits. Penny assured her she would send them up the next day, along with some other clothes to get her through until she could shop for herself.

Sheila felt bad about ordering the clothes. She still had plans to leave the city once Xavier's men found Dennis. More of her family's enemies might show up, and she didn't want them messing with her new Pack or Xavier's Court.

Thoughts of escape temporarily fled her mind once she tried on the dress. It was perfect for the statement that she wanted to make at the gala.

"No! You can't wear that." Anita looked appalled. "It's…"

Sheila smiled at the Nightshade shop owner. "It's perfect."

# Chapter Eleven

Xavier stepped out of the elevator into the penthouse a little after 3 A.M. He had left his guards down on the 30<sup>th</sup> floor. After all, there was no reason for them to come up and disturb Sheila.

"Do you normally work until the wee hours of the night?" Sheila's voice floated from the completely dark living room.

The wolf was stretched out on the sofa. She was lying under a blanket. It was clear that she was waiting for him.

"Yes. If I don't have any events planned, I've been known to work up to dawn." He locked eyes with his Shadow. Now that she was in his life, he would have to change up his work habits. He even found that he relished the idea of spending time with her.

"We need to talk." Sheila sat up, letting the blanket fall off her. She was wearing a pair of satin pajamas.

Seeing her in those pajamas made Xavier want to do something, but it wasn't talking. He made his way into the kitchen, where he set down his laptop bag. "Do you want anything before we talk?"

"No."

There weren't any strong emotions coming from her. It didn't bring him any relief, however. Their Bond wasn't in place, so relying on that to tell him her state wasn't the best thing.

Xavier left the lights out as he entered the living room. He sat on the chair across from her. "So, what's so important that you waited up for me?"

"My status here at the Tower." Sheila curled her feet onto the couch. "I need to leave before Dennis gets ahold of me."

Rage threatened to overtake Xavier at the thought of some other man touching what was his. He pushed it down. "I won't that thug touch you."

"I can't stay here. Dennis will keep causing problems as long as I'm here." Sheila turned slightly, so she was looking out of the window. He could hear the fear and stress in her voice. "I wonder how he found me." The last words were whispered into the dark.

"Look at me." The command in Xavier's voice made Sheila to whip her head back to look at him in surprise.

There was no way that she was going to leave Cleveland and live in fear of discovery ever again. She had a home now, and she needed to accept it. Now to convince her.

"If you run, Dennis will never leave you alone. I will protect you from him." Xavier moved from his chair to sit beside her on the couch. He put his arm around her and pulled her to his side.

Sheila shook her head stubbornly. "You can't just decide that for me. I won't let you or anyone else get hurt to protect me. He killed my entire family over a damn debt!" A tear rolled down her cheek.

"Sheila, You're my Shadow. I will kill to protect you." His grip on her tightened. "I'm the fucking Master Nightshade of Cleveland. No jumped-up Alpha is going to touch you."

Groaning, Sheila let her head drop to his shoulder. "Talking to you is like talking to a brick wall. Do you hear yourself? You can't just decree something and make it happen."

Xavier barked out a laugh. Did she not know that in most cases what he wanted, he got? That was part of the perks of being a Master. "Um, sweetheart, do you know who you're talking to?"

His reply had Sheila breaking out into nervous giggles. Xavier said nothing while she laughed off her tension.

"Seriously, though, Xavier. You can't just burst into my life and tell me what's going to happen. I'm a grown ass adult who's been making decisions for myself for years."

*Take a deep breath; don't yell at your Shadow.* "I understand, but you need to realize that it's not just you now. Like it or not, we will be together for the rest of our lives." Xavier looked down at the top of Sheila's head, willing his eyes not to change in response to his emotions.

Sheila rudely snorted. "Okay, then you also need to accept that if we're to be together, it can't be just your way or the highway." She lifted her head off his shoulder. "We will be partners or not together at all."

If Xavier had to be honest with himself, he didn't like her condition. But she was right. If she allowed him to, he would run roughshod all over her opinions. As the Master of Cleveland, he often made life-or-death decisions without consulting anyone. But doing that in a relationship would doom it from the start.

He took a deep breath and let it out. "You're right."

The surprise on Sheila's face amused him.

"Wow, I expected there to be more of a fight from you." Sheila grinned at him.

He tapped her nose. "But you must remain here with me. I won't risk your safety by allowing you to go back to your old apartment."

"Okay."

# Chapter Twelve

"Gorgeous!" proclaimed Penny as Sheila stood in front of a full-length mirror in the second bedroom of the penthouse.

The shop keeper had descended on the penthouse with a makeup artist, her assistants, and a hairdresser earlier in the evening. She had declared that she would supervise Sheila getting ready for her first event in Cleveland. That was to the dismay of Anita, who showed up later.

Sheila was tired of Xavier's assistant. She wondered what he saw in the human. Maybe she was efficient. Or maybe she was good at something else. But the woman was fucking annoying.

Thankfully for Sheila's peace of mind, Anita returned to work after being ignored by everyone.

Sheila couldn't believe the transformation that the team had pulled off in a few hours. She didn't look like the same wolf.

The hairdresser had blown her hair out straight and added extensions in before putting her hair up into a chignon. Emerald and diamond combs held the creation up.

Her hair was the only thing about her outfit that was elegant. The rest went toward dramatic. The make-up artist made up her face like she was on a runway. She did Sheila's eye makeup in shades of green and white with the liner done in the cat-eye effect.

But the star of the ensemble was her emerald-green silk dress. The top was two strips of silk that went from the waist to tie around her neck. Two-way tape and prayers were the only thing keeping her from having a wardrobe malfunction. The top connected to a full skirt that split on one side up to mid-thigh. A stray breeze would reveal she was wearing a thong of the same color.

She wore emerald drop earrings, and on each arm, a white gold cuff surrounded her wrists that were encrusted with emeralds. One ring adorned each hand.

"Thank you all!" Sheila turned and gave the group a wide smile. She lifted her arms wide and motioned to herself. "This is the look that I was going for."

How would Xavier react when he saw her? Sheila knew she shouldn't place so much stock in his opinion, but he was worming his way into her heart. Over the past day, he had taken time out of his day to just get to know her. And in return, Sheila was getting to know the man underneath the Master of the City persona.

"It was our pleasure." Penny picked up her tote. "Let's clear out so that they can get going."

There was a knock at the door before it opened. Xavier stood there, looking like a snack in a tailored black tux. Sheila's wolf yapped inside her in happiness.

He walked in, ignoring everyone but her. The others cleared out of his way, not even trying to hide their smiles.

Xavier circled her with an intent look in his dark eyes. "You look good enough to eat." He stopped to give her a faint smile, a hint of elongating fang peeking through.

Heat spread through Sheila's cheeks. She was so glad that her skin was dark enough that her flush didn't show. But she suspected Xavier could smell her reaction.

Sheila tapped him on the arm flirtatiously. "Let me grab my purse and we can head out." She reached over and grabbed the silver handbag that matched her silver sandals from the dressing table.

"We could stay in." Xavier took her hand in his and started out the bedroom.

"Not after all the time it took them to get me ready!" Sheila looked up at him with fake horror.

Xavier pretended to recoil. "Penny would slay me."

"And don't you forget it!" came Penny's retort from the elevator lobby.

Everyone in the penthouse laughed as the pair joined the group, waiting for the elevator. When it arrived, Xavier motioned them to enter.

"Send the elevator back up. We'll wait," he said. With smiles for the Master of the City and his Shadow, they departed.

Xavier motioned for Sheila to turn around. "Let me get a good look at you."

She turned in a slow circle, giving Xavier a full view of her outfit. "You like?"

"I more than like. What in the world is holding your dress up?"

Sheila looked down at her gown. "Two-way tape."

"I'm impressed."

"You should be. It's doing a better job than my bras normally do." Sheila looked over at the floor indicator. The elevator just got to its destination. "Why are we leaving so soon?"

"The venue is at a country club owned by the Pride. It's over an hour away with good traffic." Xavier pulled his phone from his pocket and checked the time.

"What can I expect tonight?"

The vampire put away his phone before returning his attention to her. "Everyone of importance in this area will be there. It's an event exclusive to the Supernatural world."

A trickle of doubt crept in. She was the daughter of career criminals. Her social circles didn't include the cream of society. Hell, the only reason her parents taught her proper table etiquette was so that she could steal from others. When she was a kid, her mother had visions of Sheila getting access to wealthy homes and stealing from them.

"What will we be doing there?" She was proud that her voice was even.

Xavier put an arm around her shoulder and pulled her in close. Her shoulders relaxed, and she leaned into him. "Mostly talking and showing off." He leaned down and kissed the top of her forehead. "People will be eager to meet you. I'm sure rumors of our meeting have already spread."

She let out an explosive breath. "What if I mess up somehow?"

"Who cares? No one will say anything to your face." Xavier put a finger under her chin and lifted her face, so she looked directly at him. His dark eyes studied her face. "Trust me, you'll be fine."

From his mouth to the Moon Goddess's ear that he was right.

# Chapter Thirteen

Sheila stared out the window at the brightly-lit country club. It was a massive, three-story structure. From what she could see of the manicured grounds, the members had money. She idly wondered if any humans were members. Probably not, unless they were one of the few like Anita who knew about the supernatural world.

Turning to look out the back window, Sheila noted the second truck that held three other members of Xavier's security and Anita. She tried to hold back her smile at the memory of Anita's face when she realized she wasn't riding with Xavier. The sour look she aimed at Sheila before plastering on a fake smile told Sheila most of what she needed to know. The human assistant resented Sheila's intrusion into Xavier's life.

*I wonder if she wanted to be Xavier's shadow.* That would explain her comments about what was appropriate for the Court over the past two days. Or she could just be a prude.

If she was going to stay for a while in Cleveland, she would have to speak with Xavier about her. There was no way she was going to keep putting up with Anita's oh-so-sly comments. Or better yet, she would deal with the human herself.

Xavier turned to her. "I don't know if anyone warned you, but protocol is that you'll be referred to as Sheila Blackwood because we haven't had our Bonding ceremony."

That was a surprise. "Why not by my last name?"

"It signifies that the Pack is giving you over to my Court. After the ceremony, you'll be Sheila Silversbane." Xavier put his phone into his pocket.

She frowned. "Sounds like a marriage custom."

"Well, in some aspects, a Bond is like a marriage. But you can't dissolve a Bond." Xavier opened the door to the truck and got out. Sheila wanted to continue the discussion, but his disappearing back put an end to it.

Camera flashes started going off as he reached in to help Sheila out. She wanted to respond to that last comment, but the small crowd behind a roped-off area stopped her. Most of the crowd appeared to be photographers and reporters. She sniffed the air, trying to identify their races. While the scents were mixed, she didn't smell any humans in the crowd.

She really hated people taking her picture. With a simple social media post, anyone with a grudge against her family could find her.

"Chin up," whispered Xavier into her ear.

The cameras caught the heartfelt smile that Sheila gave Xavier.

The pair slowly walked from the truck to the door of the country club. They occasionally slowed so that the photographers could take pictures of them.

The flashing lights from the camera had a headache forming behind Sheila's eyes. She wanted to yell at the photographers to stop, but she didn't. No one would know that she wasn't at the top of her game. But she couldn't stop her sigh of relief when they crossed the threshold. Her sensitive eyes quickly adjusted from the glare of flashes to the more subdued lighting inside.

The country club entry was a three-story tall room. A grand staircase swept from the center of the room up to the second floor. Above that, the third floor had a balcony that overlooked the center floor. To the left was a counter where uniformed staff were speaking to guests. The center and right of the room were set up like a large living room.

To the back, there were two different hallways that led to other parts of the building. Everything about the area screamed "money" in an understated manner.

The local Pride had money. Or at least, some of them did. Not all shifter groups collectively shared resources. It depended on how the Alpha and Elders ran their group.

All the attention in the room turned to her and Xavier. Sheila was acutely aware of the scrutiny, even if everyone was trying not to stare.

Her wolf wanted to hide, and Sheila couldn't blame her. Nothing good ever came of being the center of attention.

Something was niggling at her mind. Sheila looked around before she realized the feeling was in her head.

*Don't show your nerves.* Xavier's voice was inside her head.

How in the hell did he do that? *Once we Bond, you'll be able to speak back. Your ability to mind speak is minor.*

Great. Xavier could use mind speech while she couldn't. Sheila wanted to snap at him. Then, she realized that was pretty childish of her. And she hated feeling childish.

"Let's move." Xavier started walking, still holding her arm. "If we stand still, we'll be trapped by those I don't want to speak to."

Sheila spotted Brody across the room. He was talking with a wolf that she recognized as an Elder of his Pack, a woman name Elise. "There's Brody."

Xavier altered their path, neatly avoiding a dragon shifter couple. Consternation briefly crossed their serenely elegant faces.

"Who was that?" Sheila kept her voice down to a whisper.

"The Alpha of the Detroit Conclave and his mate," said Xavier in a low tone. "He's a pompous ass, but he and the Columbus Alpha are close allies."

Sheila wasn't too familiar with dragon politics. "Is there a Cleveland conclave?"

"No. The Columbus Conclave holds Northern Ohio, and Louisville has southern Ohio and the northern part of Kentucky."

She wanted to ask more, but they had reached Brody and Elise. The Alpha smiled broadly at them. Elise was more reserved but was also happy to see them. They quickly exchanged greetings.

"Have you set a date for the Bonding ceremony?" asked Elise.

"Not yet." Xavier glanced around briefly at the crowd. "I have to inform Andre and see when he can come down here."

And what Xavier didn't mention was that he and Sheila hadn't come to an agreement that she would stay. She was only there for a week before she could leave. She bit down on the urge to point that out. It wouldn't do her any good to start an argument with Xavier in front of hundreds of people. Regardless of Xavier's opinion, the option to flee was still on the table for her.

"Sheila, if it's alright with you, I'd like to do the adoption ceremony for the Pack before the Bonding." Brody's eyes met hers.

Her heart started pounding. If she accepted, she would actually belong to his Pack. Sheila looked from Brody to Xavier to Elise. All three stared back at her solemnly.

All of her life, she wanted to belong to a pack. She wanted the safety and feeling of belonging that she lacked growing up. To her, pack life represented everything that she desired out of life.

If she said yes, her dreams would come true.

She turned to Xavier with questions in her eyes. He locked gazes with her.

*This is your choice.*

But if she accepted, what would happen with Dennis? Would he destroy the pack that she was coming to love?

*Take Dennis out of the equation. The only wolf this concerns is you.* Xavier took her hand in his. Sheila was surprised to find her hand shaking. *Even after we Bond, you'll still be a member of the pack.*

Sheila grinned at Brody. "Yes! Thank you!"

# Chapter Fourteen

"Has Xavier Silversbane been taken off the market?", the headline on an article from a Supernatural social site read. A low growl escaped from Dennis's throat as he stared at the picture of the bitch and the Cleveland Master of the City.

How dare that jumped-up vampire interfere in his business? Dennis tossed the phone onto the seat beside him. He was currently in a car with two of his guards, just outside of the grounds where the Lionne Gala was being held.

"We're going in."

The guard in the passenger seat glanced back at him. "In two minutes. Our mole will be taking the guard post."

"Good. If we can get the bitch alone, we'll grab her."

Once they had her, he would take her back to Nevada. There, she would learn her lesson for running from him. He would enjoy the experience; she would not.

# Chapter Fifteen

The group spoke about potential dates for the adoption ceremony until others joined them. Xavier and Brody introduced the newcomers to Sheila, and then the talk moved to politics. Since she knew nothing about politics, she didn't protest as she was silently pushed to the edge of the crowd.

"Hello."

Sheila turned to see a human woman standing beside her. She was tall and dressed in a blue gown that didn't seem to fit her very well.

This was the first human other than Anita that Sheila had seen in the room. Maybe she was another of those rare humans who knew about the Supernatural.

"Hi." Sheila looked around, but no one from her group was paying any attention to her.

"You look just as lost as I feel here." The woman held out her hand. "I'm Diane."

"Sheila." Until she knew more about this person, Sheila would keep their conversation to a minimum. She inwardly shook her head but outwardly gave the woman a small smile.

"I see you came in with the Silversbane court. Are you a member?"

Damn, this chick was nosy. Sheila put on a bland expression and shook her head. "No. Are you enjoying yourself?"

Over the next few minutes, Sheila politely chatted with the human, who tried to get in as many questions as she could. She deflected the questions without snapping at the woman, even though it tried her patience. Finally, she broke free of the conversation.

"It was so nice meeting you." The woman nodded and quickly strode away.

Sheila frowned as the woman disappeared into the crowd. *What a strange woman. That was the most pointless conversation.* She gave a mental shrug and looked for Xavier.

Somehow, during their conversation, they had wound up near the back of the room, near the hallway. Her feet hurt, and she wanted to sit down. But she wanted to see where Xavier ended up before she found a seat.

A man stood a few feet away, looking at her. Something about him made Sheila's skin crawl.

*Yep, it's time to move from this spot.* With all the people in the room, she couldn't smell what he was.

Before she could take two steps away, he was by her side. She could smell his wolf, even though he had liberally doused himself with cologne.

And he didn't smell of Brody's pack.

"If you make a sound, I'll kill you right here." The strange wolf pitched his voice low so that no one else could hear him.

"Diane did a good job getting you away from the vampire."

Sheila froze. Her heart hammered, and her palms started sweating.

"You've caused me enough problems. Come quietly and your punishment for running away from me will be less severe." A hand grabbed her arm.

This must be Dennis. Although every wolf in Vegas knew who he was, this was her first time seeing him face to face. Sheila pushed down the panic that threatened to overtake her. If he got her outside, she was in trouble.

*"If your attacker is larger and stronger than you, your feet will be your best friends."* The memory of her father's voice played back in her mind. *"Surprise your attacker and run like hell."*

Sheila stomped down with her heel as hard as she could on his foot. Dennis swore and released her arms.

She shot off like an arrow. "Xavier!"

Eyes all over the room turned her way. Sheila didn't pay too much attention to them; she was trying to get away from Dennis.

"Here!" Xavier's voice was over on the other side of the room. Sheila ran directly to where he was talking a group of Nightshade and Magicians.

"What's wrong?" Xavier grabbed her arms.

"Dennis! He's here!" Her voice was a near screech.

Xavier's eyes flashed yellow. "Where?" Sheila pointed back to where she had been standing. He was gone.

Brody appeared beside them. "I heard." There was another of the pack behind him. "Guard Sheila."

The Pack Alpha and Nightshade turned and pushed their way through the partygoers. She watched them nervously as they disappeared into the hallway at the back.

"Did you get hurt?" asked the guard who had been left behind.

Sheila shook her head. "No." She was trying to calm her racing heart.

That had been a close call. If they hadn't been in a public space, Dennis might have kidnapped her. She would be stuck by Xavier's side or with a guard for the rest of the event and any other time she left the Tower until they captured Dennis. The thought was positively dreadful. She missed her freedom already.

The next twenty minutes were nerve-racking for Sheila as they waited for Brody and Xavier to return with word on what happened. Sheila was positive that they wouldn't catch Dennis. Because that would mean that the nightmare would be over.

Various partygoers tried to fish for information under the guise of concern for her. That caused her mood to swing from terror to irritation. And that irritation was close to turning to rage if the party-goers didn't stop trying to needle them for gossip. She had to keep telling herself that it wouldn't be politically wise to kill a guest of the Lion Pride.

The wolf who was with her glared at the nosy people, but most ignored him.

Finally, she spotted Xavier's tall figure striding towards them. He was alone. People instantly parted for him when they saw the thunderous expression on his face.

"He escaped." Xavier's voice was flat. He turned to the guard. "Brody wants you to join him in the security office."

The guard nodded and took off. Xavier glared at the surrounding crowd, and suddenly, they had a space around them.

"Are you okay?"

Sheila shallowly nodded. "I've been better." Now that Xavier was with her, she could breathe easier.

He leaned into her so that his lips were against her ear. "We can leave."

She really wanted to leave, but then that asshole would win. Something cracked inside of her. She would be damned if she would spend the rest of her life running from her problems. Remaining at the gala would be the first way to say "fuck you" to Dennis.

"No." Sheila looked Xavier dead in the eye. "We came here for a good cause. And that asshole isn't going to stop that."

For a second, Xavier just searched her eyes. He must have found what he was looking for. "Good."

The crowd parted briefly to allow Anita through. The assistant was frowning. "Xavier, what happened?" She stopped in front of them.

Sheila tried to smother a sigh. She really didn't feel like dealing with Anita. For such a hotshot assistant, how in the world did Anita miss the excitement?

"We'll discuss it later in private," said Xavier firmly. "Please let Pierre know that we're staying."

Anita looked as if she swallowed something sour but nodded. She turned stiffly and walked away.

The assistant's departure was some signal to the crowd, and they pressed in once more. Sheila put on a fake smile and played her part as Xavier's consort once more.

# Chapter Sixteen

"**Y**ou are living large, girlfriend!" Lena dramatically flung herself down on the couch.

Two days had passed since the gala. Sheila had spent both days in the penthouse while Xavier and his people searched Cleveland for Dennis. The couple hadn't had much time to spend with each other as a result.

Xavier had seen that she was going stir-crazy from being inside and suggested that she invite Lena over.

Sheila sat on a chair across from her friend. "This is a glorified prison. I can't go anywhere because they haven't found Dennis."

"Trust me when I say that you aren't the only person who wants a piece of him." Lena shifted positions until she was comfortable. "His thugs are still harassing the Pack."

They both knew why Dennis was stalking Sheila. But no one knew why he was trying to cause trouble for the local Pack.

With Dennis essentially invading another Pack's area, the wolf shifters considered him a danger to all Packs. And the Council of the Moon wouldn't blink an eye at Brody killing him. They did not encourage Packs to invade each other. In fact, they severely punished those that tried.

So why risk this action? "There has to be something that we're missing."

"What are we missing?" demanded Xavier.

He was in a conference room with Damien, Brody, and Brody's second, Paul. They were meeting to discuss the situation with Dennis.

Damien let out a long breath. "What is he gaining by harassing your Pack?"

"He's trying to make me look weak," said Brody, rubbing his hand over his chin. "I wonder if he actually has the balls to take the Pack by force?"

Xavier shook his head. "That last move would be suicidal." The Council of the Moon would crucify him if he succeeded. The Council abhorred chaos amongst the Packs.

"There's something else at play here," said Paul slowly. At first glance, one would wonder how he climbed the ranks to become second. The man was short and of slim build. But that slight stature hid the fact that he was one of the best fighters and tacticians of his Pack.

Brody looked at his second. "What do you mean?"

"All the intel on Dennis shows that while he's a criminal through and through, he's not suicidal." Paul picked up his phone and read something on the screen. "No Pack exists in the Vegas area because the Council isn't thrilled that the main Nightshade Court is based in Vegas."

Xavier knew that. The only shifter groups that called Las Vegas home were the dragons and lions. And both groups were strongly allied with Queen Sascha.

"We all know that," muttered Brody.

"How did Dennis know where to find Sheila? And check this out. Right before Sheila's family was murdered, a wolf from Spain flew into Las

Vegas." Paul looked up from his phone. "He only stayed two days and then flew out."

Brody and Xavier stared at each other. Both faces showing dawning horror.

Only one entity in the world wouldn't care about disrupting the Supernatural world. That same individual would gain an advantage from it.

Raphael, the Mad King of Europe. The ancient Nightshade was on a quest to take over the entire Supernatural world before turning his attention to the normal human world.

Brody beat Xavier to speaking. "Fuck, not the Mad king." No Supernatural wanted him in their country. His current reign was brutal.

Damien's sour look deepened. "That would explain the reckless nature of the actions the Alpha has taken."

Instead of letting dismay or other such useless emotions take over, Xavier stared off into space.

The others, recognizing the far-off look in Xavier's eyes, quieted and let him think in peace.

What would Raphael gain from destabilizing Cleveland? Xavier was under no illusion about the status of his territory in the Nightshade Court. His Court, while one of the richest, was also one of the smallest and politically weakest in North America.

The current Queen ruled over all of North America. Cleveland was under Lord Andre Silversbane, who controlled the Midwest.

Unless Raphael was trying to get back at Andre. Well, Andre's Shadow had spirited away a major artifact from right under the Mad King's nose.

"We need to catch Dennis." The three men in the room with him looked startled.

Brody was the first to recover. "How do you suggest we do that?"

"How?" Xavier's answering grin was chilly. "By setting a trap, of course."

"How'd you get so good with a gun?" asked Lena as Sheila handed the gun back to the attendant and came out of the alley.

When Lena mentioned the Tower had a shooting range in the basement, Sheila called Tim to ask about it. The guard had quickly offered to make the arrangements.

Within the hour, he had escorted the pair to the range. The manager of the range checked them out on their knowledge of weapons and got them set up.

Sheila came to stand beside her friend. "My brothers. They were determined that I could defend myself."

Tim looked satisfied. "Since you know how to handle a gun, I'll see about getting you one."

As much as she knew her way around guns, Sheila was still hesitant about carrying one. She scrunched her face up. "I'm not sure I want my own."

"You don't have to carry it out all the time, but there will be times when everyone is armed." Tim gave her a steady stare while talking. "That's part of life in a Nightshade Court."

There was the root of the problem. She didn't ask to become part of Xavier's Court. She certainly didn't ask for her family to be killed for their actions and send her fleeing for her life.

Goddamnit, she wanted to choose how her life went. Not to be swept along. But she didn't say that to Tim. He didn't deserve to be dumped on.

"It's better to have it and not need it," commented Lena, pushing away from the wall where she'd been standing. "After all, that bastard Alpha is still out there."

"He's about the only person I would shoot without hesitation." If it took putting a bullet between Dennis's eyes to free herself from him, she would do it. It would be worth it to have her life back. Then, she could concentrate on finding out if her pull towards Xavier was real or not. And if it was, a chance to have an actual relationship that wasn't tainted by her family's criminal past couldn't be missed.

"That's good to know."

Sheila turned around in surprise to see Xavier standing there. *How had he sneaked up on her?*

"How do you do you sneak up on me all the time?" Sheila walked over and leaned against him.

Xavier put an arm around her and gave her a quick hug. "Skills." He turned them so that they were facing Tim and Lena.

"Lena, your uncle is waiting for you at valet. Tim, would you mind escorting her?"

"Not a problem, sir. Will you be heading back to the penthouse?"

"Yes," said Xavier.

"I'll call you tomorrow," said Lena, picking up her purse and slinging it on her shoulder.

"Sounds good. Tell everyone at the club I said hi." Sheila missed her coworkers. She hadn't been at The Howling Wolf long, but they had taken her in at her lowest point.

Tim and Lena left before them. The manager of the range stopped her and Xavier to have a few words.

Sheila waited and listed in silence as Xavier spoke with the man. She realized Xavier regularly spoke with the tenants of the tower. It was a relief to see that he wasn't a standoffish leader. She had heard rumors of other Nightshade leaders who ranged from aloof to downright nasty.

Finally, the conversation wound down, and they parted from the manager.

"Are you hungry?"

Her stomach chose that moment to growl. She laughed awkwardly. "Yes."

Her vampire lover gave her a charming grin. "Why don't we find you something to eat? Afterward, I'm sure that we could find something entertaining to do." Xavier's eyes left no question of what he wanted.

For a moment, butterflies had replaced the empty feeling in her stomach and in her chest. Sheila searched his eyes before lowering her gaze. Xavier put his arm over her shoulder and led her toward the elevators.

# Chapter Seventeen

The next evening, Sheila found herself in a small antechamber to one of the ballrooms in the Tower. She was sitting with Penny, waiting to be introduced to the Cleveland Nightshade Court.

"What is taking so long?" Sheila glanced at the door to the small antechamber.

Penny shrugged. "I don't know. This is just the Informal Court. So, there won't be the playing of politics." She stood up. "Let me go see."

She came back a moment later. Her face was set in grim lines. "The Court is just arriving."

That statement had turned Sheila's nerves to irritation. Anita had rushed them down to this small room. The assistant had insisted that Sheila was late, causing Penny to rush to finish her makeup.

"That..." started Sheila, but stopped when Penny shook her head.

"We both know she's trouble," said Penny quietly. "Don't cause waves. Wait until after your Bonding ceremony."

The logic in that made sense, but Sheila was tired of the snarky human assistant. What did she think she was going to accomplish?

"She's going to trip herself up with Xavier eventually," continued Penny, heading back to her chair.

"Not soon enough," muttered Sheila darkly.

"Well, right now, she's Xavier's right hand in his business. That pretty much makes her unassailable until she does something stupid." Penny settled back in her seat. "Others have tried to knock her from her spot and failed."

A knock sounded at the door and then opened. Tim stuck his head in. "Master Xavier is ready for you."

Both women stood up. Penny gave Sheila a last inspection.

For the introduction, Sheila opted for a simple, blue dress that she accented with a long string of pearls and blue sandals. Penny's jeweler friend had loaned her the pearls for the occasion.

The stylist had styled her hair to highlight her curly hair. How the stylist had made it look elegant, Sheila did not know.

"You'll do," Penny teased as she motioned for her to precede her.

Sheila was grateful that the Nightshade was with her. She knew that if she had been left alone, her nerves would have sent her running.

The antechamber where they'd been waiting was across the hall from the ballroom. They were on the third floor of the Tower. For this and other Court events, security limited access to the floor to members of the Court and those who were invited guests.

Tonight's event was only for high-ranking Court members. Xavier wanted it to be a smaller event so she would be comfortable.

Tim opened the door for her. Sheila gave him a grateful glance before walking in.

The first thing that jumped out at Sheila when she entered was the level of power in the room. Nearly every being in there radiated pure, unrestrained power.

The twenty Nightshade in the ballroom were the most powerful of Xavier's Court. About half of those had their Shadows with them.

All conversation stopped when she entered the room. Sheila tried not to grimace at that. She paused, looking for Xavier. He was standing at the head of the room with his second in command, Damien, beside him. He looked quite handsome in dark dress pants and a crisp white shirt. Simple and elegant. Xavier always kept his clothing simple.

He beckoned for her to join them. She took a deep breath and forced her suddenly racing heart to calm down. By taking the next step, she was declaring to his top people that she was his Shadow. There would be no stepping away or hiding if she acknowledged his claim.

Xavier's eyes locked with hers. Concern and something else swam in the dark eyes. Then, she saw it. Acceptance for who she was. He knew her history and still wanted her.

Her wolf howled in acceptance within her. The wolf wanted what was being offered to her. She wished she agreed with her wolf. Sheila started walking slowly toward him.

As she passed the fashionably-dressed crowd, a lion shifter winked at her. He, along with two other lions who looked exactly like him, wore nothing but leather pants and a leather collar. The leather collars had chains attached that were being held by a female Nightshade.

Sheila tried not to stare at the tall, blonde Nightshade. She wore a black, tailored pants suit, with a red blouse underneath and red-soled black pumps. The lions, who were obviously triplets, had dirty blond hair, blue eyes, and muscles for days. None of the lions looked the least bit uncomfortable with the woman holding their leashes.

Before she could feel more than a thrill of alarm, Xavier's voice chuckled in her mind. *The lions are Nivea's Shadows. They are in the BDSM lifestyle and live it full time.*

Sheila knew Xavier could read her thoughts, even if she couldn't project them. He had better not think she would put up with wearing a collar.

Nivea smiled knowingly at Sheila. Then a female voice sounded in her mind. *Thank you for your concern for my pets. They willingly put up with my whims.* The voice had a purr like a stereotypical sex kitten.

Cheeks heating furiously, Sheila continued toward Xavier. His mental laughter rang in his mind.

*Rest assured, Sheila, I have other kinks that you'll discover later.*

Praying that no one realized her embarrassment, Sheila took the last few steps and stopped in front of Xavier. He nodded once at her before motioning for her to stand on his other side.

Her eyes flickered over to Damien, who gave her a small smile before he returned his gaze to the crowd.

"We're here today to introduce Sheila Davis of the Blackwood Pack to our Court." Xavier paused while the crowd clapped politely. "She is formerly from Las Vegas and has recently moved to Cleveland."

Sheila tried not to react. What was he thinking? She wasn't trying to let everyone know her background.

*Honey, that cat is out of the bag. Dennis knows you're here. And after the gala and the dress you wore, so does the rest of the Supernatural world.* Xavier's mental voice sounded faintly amused.

*But still...*

Xavier took Sheila's hand and brought it to his lips before returning his gaze to the Court. "We met at The Howling Wolf, and I knew the moment I saw her that the Goddess had blessed me with a Shadow." Again, the Court clapped, but this time, there was more feeling to it.

"Once our Bonding ceremony is complete, Sheila will be my true Consort and rule this Court by my side. Please give Sheila a warm welcome."

Everyone in the room stood, still clapping and cheering. Well, everyone except for Anita. The assistant stood at the rear of the crowd, glaring daggers at Sheila. When Sheila met her eyes, she quickly smoothed her face into a pleasant expression and clapped politely.

*Oh, sweetie. You're fucking with the wrong one.* Sheila kept staring directly at her until she looked away. It was game on. The human would find her games turned right back on her.

Once everyone settled down again, Damien announced that the formal Court was over and that if there were any petitions, Xavier would hear them at the next full Court. Several Nightshade pressed close to talk with Xavier.

Sheila took a step back to allow him to address one vampire that reminded Sheila of an old aristocratic British lord, complete with muttonchop sideburns and beard. She desperately wanted to ask him if he was from the Victorian era, but she kept her mouth closed.

A tap on the shoulder had Sheila turning around. One of the lion triplets was standing behind her. She gave him a wary smile.

He held out his hand. "I'm Brandon, one of Nivea's Shadows."

She took it. "Nice to meet you. I'm Sheila."

He pointed to his brothers, who were standing a short distance away, talking to a Magician. "Those are my brothers, Bryan and Bruce."

"Your mother stayed with the Bs in naming you three?" Sheila wanted to slap a hand over her mouth. That was not smooth at all. Where did her brain go?

Brandon snorted before barking out a laugh. "You can say that. Multiple births are common in my mom's old Pride. They had a tradition that twins and triplets had to have names, starting with the same letter."

She felt disquiet at the mention of a pride tradition. Yet one more thing that she didn't grow up with. She pushed it to the back of her mind. Now wasn't the time to feel sorry for herself that she didn't grow up in a Pack.

"That had to be rough on your mom, raising three cubs at the same time. My mom complained about having four of us, and we were spaced apart in years." Her mom had said that four pups were hard work. It didn't help that Sheila was born much later than her brothers. But having four kids didn't stop her from being a con artist. She just added the pups into her schemes.

"My mom was a twin, so she understood." Brandon looked back over at his brothers briefly before returning his attention. "We wanted to invite you to the full moon hunt at our place after your bonding ceremony. Nivea likes to host the shifters of the Court on full moons so that we all have a safe place to shift and be together."

That sounded like fun. She didn't know if she would be allowed to run with Brody's pack after she was bonded. "If Xavier doesn't mind, I would love to."

Brandon grinned. "I'm pretty sure that he won't mind. There aren't many shifters who are Bonded here in Cleveland. But the local lion Pride and panther group won't allow those of us who are Shadows to run with them." He lost his smile briefly. "And we have one dragon attached to the Court who isn't part of a Conclave. So, the gathering is for us lost souls."

"In fact, Lord Andre's Shadow, Simone, might join us as well. She doesn't belong to a Conclave. And it's a fairly short flight for her to join us," said a deep baritone from beside her. Sheila turned to see another of the triplets standing next to her. "I'm Bryan."

"Hi, Bryan." She held out her hand to him. He took it and bowed over it. Sheila tried to stifle a giggle at his over-the-top gallantry.

Brandon just rolled his eyes at his brother's antics. "The Shadows here at Xavier's Court stick together more than at other Courts."

"That's good to know. The little that I heard about the Nightshade Courts is that the politics are brutal." According to rumor, backstabbing and intrigue were a normal part of life in the Courts.

"They are. Xavier's Court is one of the better ones," said Bryan slowly as he looked around. "But it is still wise to keep aware of the politics."

"There are those here who try to use the Shadows to influence the Nightshade. You'll recognize them soon enough." Brandon brightened up again. "But enough of the gloomy talk. Have you and Xavier decided on a date for your Bonding ceremony?"

Sheila was about to answer when Anita walked up. "No, Xavier still has to decide on a date." The assistant smiled sweetly at her.

*Game on, bitch.*

"Wow, Anita. Were you in the bedroom with Xavier and me last night? Because we were discussing dates, then." Sheila raised an eyebrow. "I think we limited the time down to two or three dates while we were trying the reverse cowgirl position."

Anita grimaced at her while Brandon snorted, and Bryan outright laughed loudly. Before the woman could open her mouth, Sheila cut her off. "Ah... no, I must have tossed out a date or two while he was downtown. No... I just screamed then."

In a room full of Supernaturals with acute hearing, no conversation was private. And it showed when a few other people in the room tried hiding smiles and laughs, while others, like Nivea, laughed out loud.

"You are so uncouth!" said Anita, her voice an angry hiss. "You will embarrass the Court."

So much for Penny's advice not to rock the boat with Anita. Well, Anita started it. It was time for Sheila to finish it.

"Sweetie. I may be uncouth, but I'm the one that the Moon Goddess chose as his Shadow." She smiled, twisting the verbal knife. "Don't you have some paperwork to push somewhere?"

The entire room fell silent. Sheila could feel everyone's attention on them. It was up to Anita now. She could admit defeat or continue to come at her. Sheila really hoped that she would come for her.

Anita opened her mouth to say something when it must have dawned on her that everyone was watching them. She glared at Sheila, who just stared back at her with a wide smile on her face. "You dirty trailer trash..."

"Enough!" Xavier strode over and stood between the two women. Sheila could feel his irritation with the two of them. She wasn't too concerned, though. There was no way he could expect her to take shit from a human in public. That would doom her introduction to his Court.

The assistant turned to Xavier. "Sir, she's a..." Anita's voice trailed off as she got a full look at his face. There was now only coldness in his expression.

Sheila decided that the silence was golden and kept her mouth closed. Let Anita dig her own grave.

"Didn't I say enough?"

"Yes, sir," she said in a low whisper.

"Head home. We'll talk once I get in tomorrow."

# Chapter Eighteen

Xavier watched as Sheila exited the bathroom wearing nothing but a towel. She looked at him as she crossed over to the closet. "I'm surprised that you're not at the office already."

He had decided not to go downstairs while she was in the shower, so he'd sent Anita a message to cancel all his meetings and to clear his calendar for the evening. He still didn't trust himself to talk to his assistant yet.

Yesterday was the first time that he had seen Anita step over the line with Sheila. A few had mentioned to him that his assistant had gradually taken on airs and manners like she was his Shadow. Last night, Damien had told him that wasn't the first time she had done it since Sheila had arrived.

Logic told him that Anita was jealous of Sheila. But he didn't see why. He never indicated to her she was ever in consideration to be his Consort. He hadn't slept with her because he didn't want the complications to interfere with their business relationship. She was an excellent assistant, and he wanted to keep their relationship business only.

But he would toss her to the side if she tried to interfere with his relationship with Sheila.

"Come here." He patted the bed beside him. "We need to talk about Dennis."

Sheila came over to the bed. She frowned at him. "That was a good way to ruin my day." She sat on the edge. He could feel the tension radiating from her.

If he could figure out a way to get rid of Dennis that didn't involve her, he would take it. The last thing that he wanted to do was endanger his Shadow. Neither he nor Brody could come up with a better plan.

"What if I told you we have a plan to flush Dennis out of hiding?"

"Oh?" She adjusted her seat, and the towel slipped down, exposing a nipple before she pulled it back up.

Xavier licked one of his fangs that had descended at the sight. One night after the bastard was captured, he would sample some of her blood from that plump breast. He forced himself to get his mind back on the task at hand. They would have plenty of time to play in the future.

"We're going to have to lure him out of hiding." He reached out and snagged her by the waist. She squeaked when he pulled her over his lap so that she lay across his lap. He started stroking her back, and she relaxed.

"How?"

"Tonight, the Pack is going to hold your adoption ceremony and a run afterwards. Brody figures Dennis will try for you then." He felt her tense, and he placed his hand her on her back to prevent her from jumping up.

"Wait. We will have Nightshade in the woods hidden by the Pack Magician to track you back to where Dennis is hiding, and we will kill him once and for all."

Sheila's body started shivering. "So, I'm the bait. What happens if he eludes the watchers?" Her voice shook as well.

Xavier could hear her fear speaking. "They won't. We will have eyes on you the entire time, as well as a tracker."

She shook her head. "You didn't hear what he said to me. He plans on punishing me for running."

It broke his heart to hear the fear in her voice. There was no way that he would let Dennis get his hands on Sheila. He didn't want to place her in harm's way, but they had to eliminate him quickly.

"He won't get you. If there was any other way to stop him, I would take it."

Sheila turned her head so that she was looking up at him. "Promise he won't get me?"

"Promise."

Xavier slipped out of the bed, leaving Sheila sleeping. He hoped that the lovemaking would tire her out for a while. She hadn't slept well since she moved into the penthouse. Maybe he would get a Magician to spell her for sleep after all of this was over.

Once out in the living room, he sat on the couch and went through the messages on his phone. There was one from Anita. She wasn't feeling well and wanted to go home. He shot off a message telling her to take the next day off as well. It would give him the time to cool off before talking to her.

Another was from Damien, asking to meet before they left for their assigned spots at the ceremony. He responded to the message and several others as well, before setting his phone down. He stared out of the window at the city skyline, thinking about everything he had to gain by this action. And what he had to lose.

# Chapter Nineteen

Sheila woke up an hour later. She was by herself in the bedroom. Listening, she didn't hear Xavier in the penthouse. He must have gone down to his office or somewhere else in the Tower.

She wished he was still with her. Being alone meant that she had plenty of time to think about the plan to capture Dennis. She really wanted Dennis to go away. It was crazy how he chased her across the country for something that her dad did. But nothing he had done since he came to Cleveland made sense.

There was no way that Dennis could not know that the Council of the Moon would soon be after him. They could not allow him to get away with his aggression towards Brody's Pack. If he succeeded in taking over the Pack, other Alphas with illusions of grandeur would start taking over other Packs.

Running was still on the table. But shit, she didn't want to run now. She finally found a home and, dammit, she was going to keep it. So, that left flushing Dennis out. Fuck.

She sat up and reached over to her nightstand to grab her phone. There were no messages to distract her from her thoughts. And she didn't feel like browsing Facebook or TikTok.

*I might as well shower again. I'm not going to the ceremony smelling of sex and Xavier.* There was no need for her to advertise the fact that she shared a bed with the Master of Cleveland. No matter that everyone assumed it, she didn't want to prove it true.

Twenty minutes later, she was in the kitchen fixing a snack when her phone rang. She picked up the phone. "Hello."

"Miss Davis? It's David from security."

"Yes?"

"There is a package here for you. Would you like me to send it to the penthouse?" asked David.

"Sure." She thanked the man and hung up the phone. It must be some of the clothing she ordered from Penny.

As she finished her snack, the ring tone that signified someone was on the private elevator sounded. Sheila put her dishes into the sink and went to the elevator lobby.

The elevator opened, and a security guard stepped out. He held a manilla envelope in his hands along with a tablet. "Miss Davis, can you sign for this?"

Sheila took the tablet that he offered her and quickly used her finger to sign for the envelope. She exchanged the tablet for the envelope, and the security guard entered the elevator again and left.

She stood there in the lobby, staring at the envelope. It didn't have a return address on it. Someone addressed it to her at the Tower. Who had sent it to her? She held the envelope up to her nose to sniff it. None of the scents on it were familiar to her. It was a long shot, anyway.

She ignored the little voice in her head, telling her to talk to Xavier before opening the package.

"I might as well open it." Sheila ripped it open while she walked back into the living room. She flopped down on the couch and pulled out the contents.

Inside were a couple of pages of what appeared to be a report and some pictures of Sheila's brother, Dave. One picture was a mugshot of him from the Clark County Sheriff's office. Others appeared to be surveillance footage of him.

"What the fuck?" Sheila looked at each of the photos before setting them down beside her. She picked up the report and read.

Twenty minutes later, she was shaking. *How dare he?* Xavier must have investigated her brother and appeared to know where he was located. According to the report, he had found out the day after she moved into the Tower.

And what made that even worse was that there was a note at the end, that Dave would not be allowed to contact her for any reason without Xavier's permission. That note had Sheila seeing red.

Why hadn't Xavier mentioned to her he had found her little brother? He knew she had fled Nevada and hadn't been able to contact him. He wanted to keep her away from her last living family member?

She placed the report back into the envelope before getting to her feet to pace. Her mind was racing all over the place. Did Dave know she was safe in Cleveland? Why had he remained in Nevada? Was he safe from Dennis's goons?

The tone in the lobby rang out again, informing her that someone was on their way up. She hoped it was it was Xavier. He had some serious explaining to do, and it had better be good.

His scent drifted into the room ahead of him. Xavier came in wearing black combat gear and a shoulder holster with a gun in it. It was the first time she'd seen him wear anything like it. He must have been ready to head out to the Pack grounds to get into position with his team.

The calm expression on Xavier's face slipped when he caught sight of her. He stopped a good ten feet from her. "Sheila, what's wrong?"

Sheila said nothing but pointed at the envelope lying on the sofa. She didn't trust herself to speak.

Xavier grabbed the envelope and pulled out its contents. All the expression leeched from his face. He quickly flicked through the pages and then threw them on the couch.

"Where did that come from?"

Sheila gave him a dirty look before rolling her eyes. "Fuck if I know. Is it true you've found my brother?"

For a second, it looked like Xavier would say nothing before he decided against that action. He walked over to Sheila, but she threw up her hand in a stop gesture.

"Just tell me the truth."

"Yes," Xavier said heavily. He balled up his fists and then released them.

"Then why didn't you tell me?" Sheila turned away from him, not wanting him to see the tears that were welling in her eyes. Her head was hurting from the emotional swings she had been going through.

Xavier walked up to her and put his arms around her from behind. She stiffened but didn't break free from him. "Because I didn't want him to hurt you."

"Bullshit. Why would I be hurt by knowing where my brother was?" Her voice broke on a sob. "You left orders for the Tower staff not to even admit I was here!"

She could feel him take a deep breath. "Because of what I learned about him. He would only use you once he found out about your connection to me."

"You don't know that. Dave's my little brother. He's all the family that I have left." Sheila tried to move from within his arms, but he tightened them. "Let me go, dammit!"

"Whoever sent you that envelope only shared certain parts of the report." Xavier dropped his arms from around her and stepped back.

Sheila took a few steps forward before turning around to face him. "What?"

Xavier crossed his arms, his eyes flashing yellow. "Dave never left Nevada. Why would someone afraid for their life stay in the same area that they were in danger in?" He turned and went to sit on the couch.

Not trusting herself to speak, Sheila started pacing again. After a moment, Xavier resumed.

"Your brother is still in the same area. Once the police were convinced that he had nothing to do with your family's death, he went right back to his life." Xavier paused a second before continuing. "In fact, the investigator spotted him talking to one of Dennis's bookies right before Dennis left Nevada to come here."

There was no way that her brother would betray her. Sheila shook her head. He was the one that warned her to flee. Dave loved her enough to warn her of the danger. He even told her to do Plan Z which was to just disappear.

"Stop!"

But Xavier continued without pity. "In fact, he unexpectedly came into a large sum of money recently. He's been seen at several casinos, heavily gambling as well as bragging to anyone who would listen that his sister was the Lady of Cleveland."

"You don't know how he came into that money!" The room was closing in on Sheila. She didn't want to hear anymore. "Why are you doing this to me?"

Sheila ran out of the living room and went into the second bedroom, slamming the door behind her.

# Chapter Twenty

Xavier kept an impassive expression on his face as Sheila stormed out of the room. He didn't want her to see the frustration on his face. After the door slammed, he slumped back onto the couch.

He glanced over at the damning papers on the cushion beside him. He flicked his telekinetic power lightly and sent the papers and envelope flying. *Who sent this report to her?*

There were only a couple of people who could have accessed the Tower's servers to pull it. And of those people, only one currently had the motivation to damage their relationship.

As much as Xavier wanted to go back into the bedroom with Sheila and talk, he had to let her cool down. She would need as much composure as she could get to pull off the plan.

They couldn't afford to postpone it because of the fight between the two of them. After it was all over, he promised himself that he would sit down with her and talk it out. As it was, Sheila was still a flight risk. He wasn't positive that she had given up on fleeing. And until they completed the Bonding ceremony, he couldn't hold her to him.

And losing her wasn't even an option. Sheila was now an integral part of his world that he could not deal without. If she left, part of his soul would depart with her.

Sheila was the other half of his soul. She was the person who Hecate chose for him. Once the bond was in place, he would be so much stronger than he was now.

He reached down and pulled his phone out of the cargo pocket along his left leg. He typed a quick text to Damien. *Find out who accessed the report on Sheila's brother. Someone sent part of the report to Sheila here at the penthouse.*

Xavier got up and grabbed the envelope. He swore when he saw it didn't have a return address. *Also, find out who thought it was a good idea to send an envelope without a return address directly to Sheila without security checking it out.*

His phone pinged. *Will do. You know who probably did it right?*

*Yes. But I want proof before I take action.*

*Got it.*

He pulled up Tim's number. His guard answered on the second ring. "Yes, boss?"

"I need you to come up here and stay in the penthouse until it's time for Sheila to head to the Pack grounds." Xavier stood up and started for the elevator. "Then take her over and join the rest of the crew once she's safely with Brody's enforcers."

"Yes sir. The watchers from earlier are still outside the Tower."

Xavier smiled. Something was going right. "If any of them move before you and Sheila leave, let me know."

"I'll be up in five."

He would talk with Sheila later, after the ceremony. That would give them both time to cool off.

# Chapter Twenty-One

The anticipation in the atmosphere was so thick that Sheila thought she could cut it with a knife. Members of the Pack stood around a clearing that had been lit with battery-operated lanterns. The clearing was a little way inside the wooded acres that the Blackwood Pack collectively owned.

The main Pack house was also on the property where Brody and several wolves lived. Most of the Pack lived off of Pack lands throughout the territory.

An Enforcer had escorted Sheila to the clearing from the Pack house. By design, she was one of the last to arrive. Everyone greeted her with smiles and words of welcome. The acceptance of the Pack slightly eased her concerns about the plans in place for the evening. But it did nothing for the hurt caused by Xavier's words. That hurt was lodged deep in her heart, where nothing could shake it.

"Sheila! You're here!" Lena came up with her arms open wide and gave her friend a big hug.

She returned Lena's embrace. "Well, I couldn't miss the ceremony, could I?"

"Come on over. We were just waiting for you to start." Lena grabbed her hand and pulled her over to where Brody and his second, Paul, were talking.

Brody broke off his conversation and turned to the two young women. "Good evening, Sheila." He took her hand and looked into her eyes. She saw the concern that was there.

Her wolf roused at being in the presence of her soon-to-be Alpha. Sheila could feel the wolf looking out of her eyes at the Pack. The wolf approved. It was happy that she was finally part of a Pack like nature intended.

Brody's eyes flashed to that of his wolf's for a second before returning to their normal green. "Well, I wasn't expecting your wolf to appear before the ceremony."

"Why not?" Sheila's wolf often rose within her. While the wolf rarely tried to take her over, it didn't remain dormant all the time, either.

Paul appeared to be studying her as well. "Most of the time, when a shifter isn't part of a Pack, the wolf is dormant, only rising during the full moon."

Sheila frowned. "Do you mean your wolf is constantly with you?"

"Yes. And with Alphas, the wolf is a separate personality that speaks and lives within them," said Brody quietly. "We speculate that those who don't belong to a Pack are dormant to keep the shifter from going feral."

Her stomach started roiling, and Sheila fought to keep from vomiting right there. Her parents' decision not to belong to a Pack harmed her and her brothers more than she had initially thought. Why had they decided that their lifestyle mattered more than belonging to a Pack?

She wanted to demand answers, but they were dead. And the dead couldn't explain the reasons for their decisions in life.

With some effort, Sheila forced herself to breathe. She could ponder the what-ifs and cry to the heavens, but it would do her no good. So, she would move on and think about this later.

"What are we going to do during the ceremony?"

Brody grabbed her change of topic with some relief. "After I welcome you into the Pack, I will use my power to force your change on you. This will tie you into the Pack by magic."

"Afterward, the Pack will go for a run and then meet back at the Pack house for a party," said Lena.

By this time, the other members of the Pack present had surrounded them. About fifty wolves were present, so not all were there. The children, teens, and elderly were back at the Pack house waiting for the ceremony to end. Brody had hired some Enforcers from the lion Pride to guard those back at the house. With Dennis still in the area, he didn't want them to be attacked while the ceremony was going on.

Sheila resisted the urge to look around for the vampires that she knew were watching. The Pack Magician must have done a good job with her spell since she couldn't smell any hint of them around.

"Everyone, we are here today to adopt Sheila Davis into the Blackstone Pack. She has proven by word and deed that she belongs with us." Brody wasn't shouting, but every person in the clearing could clearly hear his voice.

The crowd reacted warmly by clapping and cheering. Sheila gave them a grateful smile.

"She comes to us from Nevada and brings many skills to the table. During her weeks here, she has worked at The Howling Wolf and has helped several businesses with their finances. And everyone in the Pack who has met her likes her for her wit and charm."

The Alpha paused and looked around the crowd. "I won't bore you with a long speech. Will the Blackstone Pack accept Sheila Davis into our ranks as a full member?"

One person in the crowd started howling like a wolf, and the rest of the Pack joined in. Sheila blinked back the sudden tears that threatened to fall at their acceptance of her.

One by one, the members of the Pack quieted until the clearing was silent once more. After a few seconds of silence, the Pack started moving until they formed a large circle around Brody and Sheila.

"Once you transform into a wolf in front of me, you will belong to the Pack. Do you consent before the Pack and the Moon Goddess to allow me to force your shift?" Brody's eyes were now that of his wolf, and they were glowing yellow.

The wolf inside of Sheila was moving around inside her. She could feel its power waiting to be freed. Her own eyes bled from their normal dark brown to the ice blue of her wolf's.

"Yes." Her answer was simple yet held tons of unspoken meaning in it.

"So be it." Brody reached out and touched her face gently.

Sheila screamed as power raced from his hand into her body via her face. It felt like a lightning bolt had hit her. Her wolf started yowling in pain with her as fire raced throughout her body.

Then fur started growing out of her skin. Her body glowed with a soft white light as she slowly transformed into a silver wolf.

Normally, the transition from human to wolf was nearly instantaneous. A gift from the Moon Goddess. This time, the change was slower. And by the Goddess, it hurt! Sheila could feel her bones break and reform into her wolf shape.

Her scream turned into a howl as the transformation completed. She laid in her wolf form in a pile of torn clothing.

"The Moon Goddess has accepted Sheila into the Blackstone Pack. Prepare for the run to celebrate the expansion of our Pack." Brody's pronouncement caused cheers again.

The Alpha knelt beside Sheila. "Are you okay?"

She wearily lifted her head off her forelegs and nodded. Sheila didn't have mind speech, so she couldn't respond to him.

*I'm proud of you,* Xavier's voice said in her mind. Sheila could feel the sentiment in him. Then, alarm flashed between them. *There's about to be an...*

Someone yelled at the outskirts of the crowd, "We're under attack!"

Black-clad bodies raced into the clearing with guns and knives. Chaos took over.

Brody snarled and transformed into a very large, red wolf. He snapped at one figure that tried to head for Sheila before veering off.

Sheila stood wearily. There was no way that her new Pack was going to fight without her helping. Her wolf shook itself inside her mind and told her it wanted to take her over. Sheila willingly switched places in her mind with her wolf. Her wolf was a far better fighter in this form than she was.

Vampires started dropping onto the ground from the trees surrounding the clearing. They all wore weapons and started attacking the attackers. Meanwhile, the Enforcers of the Pack started fighting in their human forms while the remaining Pack members transformed into their wolves and went after the attackers.

Sheila was snapping and swiping at those who came after her. She was aided by the fact that they didn't appear to want to hurt her. They were trying to drive her away from the fight.

No matter how much she tried to stay within the main clearing, they slowly forced Sheila to the edge. Somehow, she was separated from Brody, and no one appeared to notice that she was being forcibly separated from the Pack.

A lunge from a man with a long knife forced her out of the clearing and into the darkness of the woods. Before she could figure out how to get away and back with the Pack, she felt something hit her rump with a sharp prick.

In her mind, she screamed Xavier's name right as her world went completely black.

The man watched as the silver she-wolf collapsed and then transformed into her human form. The drug that Dennis had given them worked like it should have.

"Let's go before someone notices she is missing."

Another man picked her up and slung her over his shoulder in a fireman's carry. The three attackers fled into the night with their prize.

# Chapter Twenty-Two

Xavier heard Sheila's terrified mental scream before it cut out. "Sheila!"

The two men attacking him flinched slightly from his sudden roar. Xavier didn't even think; he swung his hand out. Telekinetic power slammed into both men, sending them flying away from him.

Fear fueled his strike so that he didn't feel the normal power drain that using his powers in that manner caused. He tried to move past the spot that he had been in, but two other attackers joined the fight.

No one was going to keep him from helping his Shadow. This time, he aimed his strike at the first attacker's face. The force of the strike caved the man's head in. Without pausing, he punched the second attacker in the jaw. He landed on the ground, unconscious.

Before anyone else could engage him, he tore off for the outskirts of the clearing closest to the Pack house. The road was in that direction. He raced around the perimeter until he could smell Sheila. His nose wasn't as acute as a shifter's, so it took a few minutes.

There was no sign of her anywhere. A black wolf followed him out of the clearing with one of his Nightshade trailing behind.

"Can you track Sheila?" he demanded.

The wolf nodded. *I will track her.* It dashed off.

"Follow the wolf and report." The vampire nodded and took off running behind the wolf.

A few minutes later, the fight in the clearing was over. All the attackers were dead or captured. Brody walked over to him, naked and bloody from the fight. "Where's Sheila?"

Xavier growled, "She's gone. She screamed once, and then I couldn't feel her."

Brody swore briefly. "That means someone has knocked her out. Did anyone go after her?"

"One of your wolves and my guard are tracking her right now." Xavier felt like screaming to the heavens. "The rest were caught up in the fight."

The sound of feet running in their direction caused both Brody and Xavier to look off into the trees. The Nightshade guard ran up to them, slightly out of breath. "We followed the trail to the edge of the Pack grounds. From the tire tracks, they had a vehicle waiting." He took a deep breath. "We didn't catch them in time. The wolf headed to the Pack house to get someone there to see if they got any footage of a car or truck leaving the area."

The world dropped out from the bottom of Xavier's feet. Dennis had his Shadow. He fought down the bile that came up with that knowledge. Now was not the time to let his emotions get the best of him. "Are any of the attackers still alive?"

Paul came up to them. "There are a few alive. Do you want to question them?"

Xavier's eyes started glowing brightly in anger. "Yes." He walked back into the clearing, followed by Brody, Paul, and his guard. They approached two attackers being guarded by a shifter in wolf form and two Enforcers with guns.

"Where's Dennis?"

One of the men spit at Xavier and was kicked for his troubles by the Enforcer. "Watch your manners around the Master of Cleveland."

"Oh, he'll learn manners by the time that I'm done with him," growled Xavier. "And these two clowns will dance to my tune." He held up a hand that now sported three-inch nails. "Hold them down for me."

Within five minutes, the men were screaming for their lives. By the time twenty minutes had passed, one man was dead, and the other was telling Xavier everything that he wanted to know, just to stop the pain.

Xavier took a rag made from someone's ruined clothing and wiped his hands. He didn't know why he bothered. Blood covered him from head to toe.

# Chapter Twenty-Three

A loud hum startled Sheila into a partial wakefulness. The humming seemed to come from all around her. Try as she might, she couldn't rouse from the gray nothingness that surrounded her.

"She's trying to wake up. Should I dose her again?" The male voice sounded as if it were far down a tunnel. She tried reaching for the voice but couldn't quite grasp it.

"No. I want her to know who has her."

Sudden pain on her face propelled Sheila out of the gray nothingness back to reality. She opened her eyes slowly and then wished that she hadn't.

The first thing she saw was Dennis. She shook her head and realized that they were in a small jet. In the jet were Sheila, Dennis, and two other men—probably goons of his. The jet only had four seats.

She looked down and saw that someone had tied her to the seat with a rope. Had she been by herself, she could have gotten free easily. No ordinary rope could hold a determined wolf shifter. But with Dennis and his two guards right there, they could stop her long before she freed herself.

Dennis looked satisfied that she was awake. "Hello, my dear." He gave her a small smile. "I'm so glad that we're finally chatting."

The jet started moving. Sheila looked out of the window to see they were moving away from a hangar. The sky was the light twilight color that was just prior to dawn. *Where were Xavier and the others?*

Sheila looked back at him. She didn't trust herself to speak just yet.

"Ah, wolf got your tongue?" Dennis laughed and the other two men in the jet laughed uneasily with him. It was clear that they didn't find his remark funny but were just laughing because their boss was laughing.

If she wasn't scared of being killed right away, Sheila would have made a smartass comment about that. But the man in front of her was a stone-cold thug. He would kill her and then go have breakfast immediately after. She wasn't trying to die today from a comment. Better to keep quiet.

"Well, you're smart at least. I hate chatty women." He leaned forward in his seat and pointed a finger at her. "First lesson, you only speak when asked a question. The only time I want to hear from you is when I cause you pain."

She couldn't stop her eyes from widening in alarm. This man was fucking sick. She pressed back in her seat to get away from him.

He took a deep breath. "I love the smell of fear on a woman. Too bad we're on this tiny ass plane, or I'd fuck you right now."

*Keep calm*, she thought to herself. But that was easier said than done. This wolf was planning on raping her, and right now, there wasn't a damn thing she could do.

The jet taxied onto the runway. "Attention, we're about to take off. Please remain in your seats with your seatbelts on. Flight time is four and a half hours," the pilot announced over the intercom.

"We're on our way back to Vegas." Dennis's black eyes were trained on her face. "Once we're safely back, my employer will assassinate your precious Master Xavier. So don't worry about him rescuing you."

Heart pounding, she tried to stifle her protest at the thought of Xavier dying but failed. Dennis backhanded her. She slumped back against the seat, her head ringing.

"Tsk tsk." The Alpha shook his head in mock sympathy. "I told you I like my women quiet. I think I'm going to enjoy training you. If you're a good girl, I'll keep you."

He paused for a second. "If you're not, I have plenty of buyers who would love a wolf slave."

Sheila didn't make a sound. Her head was still ringing like a bell from the slap. She didn't want to invite another hit. While she would heal relatively quickly, she didn't want to spend precious energy doing so.

This Alpha was nuts. She had to figure out a way to escape once they were on the ground. If she could get away, she could take refuge with the Queen's Court. The Queen of the Nightshade would give her sanctuary since she was Xavier's Shadow.

"Knock her out."

The goon in the seat next to her pulled a cloth out of a bag that smelled strongly of chemicals. She tried to turn her head, but he grabbed her face with one hand and put the cloth over her nose and face.

The sight of Dennis smiling was the last she saw as the world went black.

# Chapter Twenty-Four

Sheila opened her eyes slowly. Her head throbbed, and her mouth felt like the Sahara Desert. She felt a pillow under her cheek.

She was lying on a cot, covered by a thin blanket. Sitting up, Sheila studied her surroundings. She was in a small, windowless room that only held a cot and a small table. The walls were a dull, institutional gray. There was a door that opened on what appeared to be a tiny bathroom.

The world spun for a second before settling back into its normal stillness. She got up and went into the bathroom. It was a tiny, crappy bathroom with a ratty old sink and toilet. But she would not complain since her bladder was full to bursting.

She came back out into the room after relieving herself and swishing some water around her mouth. There was no place to sit but the bed, so she sat down to think.

From the dryness in the air, they had to be in southern Nevada. Sheila sniffed the air, trying to see whatever she could determine about her location. There was the smell of other male wolf shifters. She thought she could smell a lone female in the mix, but it was hard to determine that.

There was no smell of cooking food anywhere in the air. She wondered if she was in a house or some sort of commercial building. That would matter if she tried to escape.

She had to get away from Dennis. There was no way that she was going to suffer meekly at his hands. From the little that she heard of his plans, staying around would not be good for her health or mental well-being. And she somehow had to warn Xavier of the attempt on his life.

The thought of Xavier caused her to swallow a sob. She tried to reach out to him, but her lack of mind-speech hindered her.

She now regretted picking that fight with him over Dave. It would haunt her for the rest of her life, knowing that their last words to each other were angry ones.

No. She would see Xavier again. And this time, when she saw him, she would tell him how she felt. There would be no more dancing around the subject. No more hiding or running. She had a glimpse of the life that being Xavier's Shadow would give her.

Even if Xavier didn't love her, she knew he cared deeply for her. They could work on their relationship with time. With the clarity of hindsight, she knew she wanted to work on a relationship with the handsome vampire.

But only if she got free of Dennis.

The door leading out of the room opened without knocking, and the goon who had knocked her out on the plane entered. He closed the door behind him. "Dennis wants to see you."

Sheila looked down at herself and realized that someone had dressed her in a thin white shift dress. She didn't want to know who had pawed at her naked body to put clothes on her.

The man looked meaningfully at the door and then lowered his voice. "He's in a foul mood. Try to say as little as possible, and you might walk out of his office without scars."

Bile rose in her throat, but she forced herself to speak. "I won't say a word unless he asks a question."

He nodded. "If you promise not to cause trouble, I won't put you into handcuffs." He patted the cuffs hanging from his belt.

"I won't cause any trouble." It would be foolish for her to run right away at that moment. She knew nothing of her situation. And he warned her about Dennis. She wouldn't repay his small kindness by fighting him. However, later, once she saw a chance for escape, all bets would be off.

# Chapter Twenty-Five

Xavier walked down the stairs to the tarmac where three, heavily tinted, black SUVs were waiting for them. He appreciated the tinted windows since it was nearing dawn, and they likely wouldn't make their destination before sunrise.

"Over here, Xavier!" A dragon shifter waved from inside one of the trucks. It was Matt, the Shadow of Queen Sascha. Xavier quickly went to the SUV.

"Hello, Matt," said Xavier as he slid inside. The inside was nicely cooled down. Even though it was around 5 A.M., the temps were still in the upper 80s. Las Vegas was a virtual furnace in late summer.

"I wish I was seeing you for normal reasons and not the kidnapping of your Shadow."

"Me too." Xavier liked the big dragon shifter. While he was growing up in the Silversbane Court, Andre would occasionally bring Xavier with him when he had business in Las Vegas. Matt had always made time to spend with the young Nightshade. He was like an uncle to Xavier.

"We'll get her back. Hold on for a second while I get everyone outside sorted out." Matt slid out the other door and walked over to some of his men to talk.

Xavier pulled out his cell phone and called Damien. His second hadn't been happy to be left behind, but he needed someone he trusted in charge while he was gone.

"Have you found Anita?" he asked as soon as Damien picked up the phone.

"No, but we have confirmation that she was seen at the airport." He heard some rustling from Damien's side of the phone. "We caught two assassins trying to get into the Tower. One killed himself before I could question him, but the other one talked after some persuasion."

"What did he have to say?" Xavier had a feeling who sent the assassins.

"Raphael had hired him to kill you. We've got the Tower on lockdown right now until we figure out if there is anyone else gunning for you." Damien didn't sound pleased, and Xavier couldn't blame him.

Sighing, Xavier rubbed his eyes. "Contact Andre and let him know what is going on. Tell him I'll call him once we have Sheila."

"Will do."

Xavier disconnected the call. He wondered why the Mad King wanted him dead. Normally, he could reason out an enemy's motive and plan counters for any move that they might make. But Raphael wasn't sane by any person's definition. Somehow, he had managed to survive the death of his Shadow, a feat no other Nightshade in history had ever accomplished.

Ever since his Shadow had been killed, Raphael had been consumed by the desire to conquer the humans and make them pay his Shadow's death.

*Why couldn't someone kill the crazy bastard*? He knew that many had tried. It was rumored that Raphael kept the heads of those that tried to kill him for trophies.

The door to the SUV opened, and Matt slid into the front passenger seat of the SUV. Then, the back door opened, and Brody got in.

Matt turned back to face them. "We're going to go to the Dragon's Flame from here. It's too close to dawn to try for Sascha's estate."

"Sounds good. Were you able to track Dennis and Sheila?" asked Xavier.

"Yes. One dragon followed them from the airport to where he is holed up. Tonight, we can retrieve your Shadow." Matt turned back to the front.

"Thanks for doing that, Matt," said Brody. "I know the Conclave did what they could."

Matt gave off a snort. "If this didn't have the potential to blow up into a political nightmare, the Alpha would have ordered the Enforcer who tracked them to attack."

All the shifter Councils avoided getting involved with each other's problems. Inter-species politics was a beast at the best of times. At their worst, there could be wars. Then add to the mix, the shifter that was central to the problems was attached to the Nightshade courts, and the situation became explosive.

"Trust me, your Enforcer has my gratitude," said Brody gratefully. "The Council of the Moon wants Dennis's head. If we don't kill him, they will send a team to take him out."

There was a beep of a horn from one of the other SUVs, and then the three vehicles started driving.

Normally, Xavier loved to stare out of the windows and see what changes were made between visits. No matter how old he was, he never grew tired of seeing the strip. This time, his mind was caught up with worry for his Shadow and the mission ahead.

"Let's try to avoid that. Sascha won't be happy with the Council invading her area," said Matt.

"I'm surprised she hasn't sent someone to take him out already," admitted Brody.

Xavier didn't turn from his absent viewing of the upcoming Las Vegas Strip. "Because Sheila hasn't bonded to me yet, she can't preemptively act."

"And she's giving Xavier the opportunity to take care of the problem," said Matt, interrupting him. "I'll be tagging along to make sure that there are no other crimes against the Nightshade Court."

There was something else that Matt wasn't saying. But he wouldn't air private Nightshade concerns in front of the Cleveland wolf Alpha. As friendly as Xavier and Brody were, that wasn't the norm between Nightshade and wolf shifter. He would talk to Matt later.

"How far is the location where Sheila is being held from here?" Xavier wanted to get to the planning of her rescue. They could talk politics after it was over. He wanted to rush there now, but it would be suicide for him so close to dawn. He wished that he could reach out to her via mind speech, but without their Bonding being completed, she was just too far away.

"About forty minutes out," answered Matt promptly. "It's currently under observation by a couple of Enforcers and their apprentices. If she's moved before nightfall, we'll know about it."

He hated it, but their party needed sleep. All of them had been going for over twenty-four hours. While Nightshade could fight the need for rest for days, it wasn't good for them. Their natures made them sluggish during daylight hours.

"Good. I want to be on the road at dusk. I'm afraid that he'll move her if we wait any longer."

# Chapter Twenty-Six

Sheila looked around as she followed the goon down a long, bare hallway. It looked like they were in a large house, but not one that looked as if someone had made it a home. The walls had nothing on them and were painted a basic beige. The doors leading from it were the cheap builder-basic things that you saw in rentals.

They went up a flight of stairs, and the decor improved. The walls were still beige, but someone clearly painted it in better paint. There were expensive-looking paintings on the walls. All the doors were expensive ones. They stopped at a set of double doors.

After knocking, the goon took Sheila's arm and opened the door. Once open, he shoved her inside and then closed the door quickly.

Sheila stumbled and caught herself before she fell on her face. As she stood up, she saw she was in an expensively decorated office. It had to be at least 300 square feet of space. Her dirty feet sank into the plush, red carpet.

Wallpaper made of cloth covered the walls. There were so many paintings crammed onto the walls that they were competing for space. And at the center of the room was a massive, antique wooden desk.

Sitting at the desk was Dennis. And to her utter surprise, Anita was standing beside him dressed in a skimpy red dress that left little to the imagination. *What in the hell was she doing in Las Vegas?*

Then it clicked in Sheila's mind how Dennis seemed to always know where she was at. It hadn't dawned on her that someone inside of Xavier's organization was feeding him information.

"You stupid bitch," she growled, taking a step forward. Sheila wanted to smack the smug grin off Anita's face.

Looking between the two of them, Dennis barked a laugh. "Anita, dear, she isn't too happy to see you."

Anita gave her a gloating smile, her blue eyes glinting in the light. "Oh, dear. You actually survived the trip here. I hoped that the poison would kill you."

All the fear that Sheila had felt since Dennis kidnapped her burned away with the onset of rage—rage that this petty little human bitch set her up. And that she betrayed Xavier's trust. For what fucking gain? How long had she been working with Dennis?

She felt her fangs grow in her mouth. Her wolf was closer to the surface and ready to take over if needed. "You better hope the Alpha here protects you." Her fangs distorted her words.

Dennis reached out and ran his hands up and down Anita's arm. The human purred like a kitten and leaned into him. He pulled her onto his lap and started pawing her.

The scene positively disgusted Sheila. It took all her willpower not to leap over the desk at him. She wouldn't get far. Her body was weaker because of the poison and lack of food. All she would do was get hurt.

"Why don't you tell her why you betrayed her?"

Anita spread her legs so that Dennis could access the area between them. Sheila tried not to gag. The human giggled.

"You had no business coming into Xavier's life and taking my place. I should have been his Shadow, not some trailer park trash. I spent years helping him." Anita's eyes took on a slightly manic cast. "He was mine."

She moaned as Dennis's hand disappeared up her dress. The scent of her lust filled the room.

"When Xavier told me about you, I wanted to kill you. But there was no way that I could pull it off." She gasped and then smiled brightly before continuing. "Then, when I was heading home that night, I was approached by one of Dennis's men.

"We met after a phone call and negotiated that I would feed him information, and then he would get me out of Cleveland and set me up here in Las Vegas." She squirmed as Dennis's hand moved faster under her dress.

Dennis looked at Sheila as he brought the woman off. Anita gave a high-pitched squeal as she orgasmed on his hand. He pulled his hand out and moved it to Anita's lips. The woman sucked her juices off his fingers as if she were giving a blow job.

"Anita has been such a help to me. As a treat, I promised her she would be allowed to torture you when I started your training sessions."

Over her dead fucking body would either of them touch her. Sheila tried not to react, but her face gave her away. Dennis just laughed. "You don't have a choice. Your father stole from me, and your precious brother owes me money. I own you, bitch."

"That has nothing to do with me," said Sheila. "I owe you nothing."

Dennis's eyes grew hard. "That's where you're wrong." He dumped Anita onto the floor. The stupid woman landed with a thump and a yowl. He got up and walked around the desk to her.

He thrust his power out, and it slammed into her. She recognized what it was—an attempt to dominate her. What a fucking Alpha thing to do. Sheila resisted it and pushed back herself.

Dennis looked surprised for a second before the look morphed into anger. "How dare you defy me?" He stopped in front of her and raised his hand.

Well, there went the useful advice that the goon had given her. Too bad she was too fucking stupid to take it. All because he was a fucking bully. The backhand that followed sent her crashing to the floor. He followed her down and hit her a few more times in the face.

A loud crash followed by the shouts drew everyone's attention to the window. Dennis strode over to the window and started cursing. "How in the hell did they find us?"

Sheila took the opportunity to scoot on her rear towards the door. The bruises on her face ached. But now that Dennis was no longer hitting her, they were healing. Once she got to the door, she used it to get on her feet again.

*Baby, are you there?*

*Xavier!* She had never been so happy to hear a voice more than his. He came for her.

"Who found us?" Anita rushed over to the window and looked out. She must have recognized someone outside. "Oh, no! I'll be lucky if he just kills me."

*Are you near Dennis? Try to get away from him if you can.*

The goon from earlier burst into the room. "We're under attack, sir. We need to get you to safety."

Dennis turned away from the window. "That Nightshade is out there. He's not going to let this go. Is our visitor still in the house?"

"Yes."

"Let him earn his keep. Send him out to deal with that Nightshade," ordered Dennis sharply. He glared at Sheila. "I should just kill you now."

Sheila just looked back at him impassively. This so-called Alpha's luck was over. All she had to do was survive long enough to see him die. "You might live if you surrender."

"If I die, it's because of you! I wouldn't be here if you hadn't appeared!" Anita rushed at her with her hands raised.

Sheila didn't even hesitate. She launched herself at the stupid woman. Before Anita could take two steps, Sheila swiped out and tore her throat out with fingers that grew three-inch claws.

Anita grabbed at her ruined throat with her hand and then collapsed on the carpet. No one moved as she choked on her own blood. It seemed like an eternity, but, in reality, was only about thirty seconds before the light dimmed in her eyes.

"You just saved me having to put up with the silly bitch." Dennis's voice was indifferent. That just multiplied the horror of the situation to Sheila. "Too bad I didn't fuck her a few times before you killed her."

The house shook violently. Everyone looked around the room at each other, wondering what the hell happened. Then they heard a male voice with a Spanish accent call out, "Xavier! Greetings from the King of the Nightshade."

Dennis went back to the window and peeked out. "That bastard blew my front door out into the yard! He's going to pay for that."

Sheila thought that should be the least of Dennis's worries, considering that there was an angry Nightshade gunning for him. He really should be concerned with running away.

The goon looked at her and motioned slightly for her to move to the side of the room. She did so since it would put her further away from Dennis. "Sir, we need to get you out of here."

"I'm pretty sure that the estate is surrounded." Dennis continued peeking out of the window.

"We can take the back way via wolf form." The goon looked exasperated. In other circumstances, she might have felt bad for him having to guard an idiot. But that was his choice. He could have chosen some other life to live other than working for a wannabe mob boss with fur.

"No. Let's see if who wins the fight between our guest and that intruder. When Xavier loses, his men will be demoralized, and we can take them out."

*Sheila.*

She tried not to look around for the voice that sounded in her head. It wasn't Xavier.

*This is Matt. I'm Queen Sascha's Shadow.* The voice seemed to be some distance away. *Xavier is about to fight another Nightshade. He's going to need your help.*

*How can I help?* Sheila tried to project her mental voice but wasn't sure if she managed it. She didn't have the natural gift.

*He needs your wolf's help. Normally, if you were bonded, she would be able to reach out to help him. But you're not.* Matt's mental voice paused. *I can link your wolf to him. She will lend him some of your energy and her senses. Do I have your assent?*

*Yes!*

*I'd advise you to sit if you can. The first time can be rough.*

Sheila slid to the floor. The goon looked in her direction, but once he saw she was only sitting down, he turned his attention back to his boss and the window.

The wolf inside of her prowled to the surface of her skin. Sheila could feel her asking for permission to take over. She granted it.

Her power and strength suddenly flowed out of her. Now she understood why Matt warned her to sit down. If she had been standing, she would have collapsed to the floor.

She noticed that the scents of the house were diminished like someone had stuffed her nose up. And she had a hard time hearing what was going on outside of the house. A moment prior, she had heard everything clearly.

*I wonder if this is how humans go through the world.* She wanted to close her eyes, but she didn't dare take her attention away from what was going on. All her remaining energy was being spent to keep her upright.

# Chapter Twenty-Seven

"Perimeter clear!" Xavier heard in his earpiece. He was hiding behind a car about two houses down, while his men and Brody's
Pack worked to clear the guards outside of the house.

Brody was leading this operation since he had more tactical experience
than Xavier had. Xavier was there to spirit Sheila away and handle any
Nightshade who might be stupid enough to have joined forces with Dennis.

Intelligence suggested that one of Raphael's Court might be present. If
that was true, then Xavier was going to deal with the asshat. The statement
had to be made by a personal representative of Sascha's that she would
brook no interference in her lands.

And he would deliver the statement with some interest. No one came
and fucked with his Court. Cleveland and its surroundings were ruled
by him and him alone. No jumped-up Alpha or sycophant of Raphael's
would take that from him. Or worse yet, harm Sheila.

Two of the shifters started towards the front door of the house. They had
almost reached it when the front door blew off the house. Xavier could feel
the Power used to accomplish it.

*Oh so, Raphael's lackey is still here.* Xavier smiled to himself grimly. It was time for some action. He put his hand to his earpiece. "Fall back. That was the Nightshade. I'll handle him."

He heard the answering responses in his ear. Standing up, he slipped into the darkness. True night was his element. As a Master, he could blend into it and no one other than an equally strong or stronger Nightshade could see him.

The Nightshade stepped out of the house. The vampire was a short, heavily muscular Spaniard with dark, curly hair. He was dressed simply in dark pants and a shirt. He had a sword strapped across his back. His eyes glowed yellow in the dim light. "Xavier! Greetings from the King of the Nightshade."

He decided that releasing the darkness from around him would be stupid. He would not give the Underworld wolves a nice juicy target to shoot at. "I'm afraid that I don't know your name."

"You can call me Juan." He stepped down from the porch to the paved walkway leading up to it.

"Well, Juan, why have you come to Las Vegas? You don't have permission from Queen Sascha to be in her area." Xavier probed out with his power. He could feel that Juan had to be near his level of power. He wondered if the man had a Shadow.

"I don't need your precious Queen's permission to do anything." He looked around before returning his attention back to Xavier. "She doesn't dare do anything to me in fear of Raphael's wrath."

Xavier's jaw nearly dropped open. No, this man couldn't be that stupid. Sascha would kill him as easily as she breathed. And then send his head back to Raphael with a blistering message attached to it.

A small crunch alerted Xavier to his danger. He dropped to the ground as a knife flew over his head. He rolled over and saw a woman standing behind him, drawing another knife. She crumpled as a gun went off. One of his guards shot her in the chest.

"Nice try, Juan." Xavier stood up, brushing the dirt off his combat gear. "Do you want to come quietly to face Sascha?" He could feel the others behind him waiting for the chance to act.

Juan scoffed. "Why would I do that? We have your pretty Shadow in the house. If I give the word, she's dead."

"And if you do that, you're dead. You'll be filled with lead before the last word left your mouth." Xavier took a step forward. "This isn't your fight. The Council of the Moon has found Dennis guilty of his crimes in Cleveland."

Juan casually started heading for him. "You're right. I'm here for you. Dennis was just a pawn in the game." He raised his hands up beside his head. "I challenge you to the death."

"Since you called a challenge, I choose power and claw as weapons." Xavier's eyes started glowing with the challenge. His power rose in him as he called upon it. And then something unexpected happened. Power from outside of him poured into him.

*You're in Sascha's territory.* Matt's voice whispered into his mind. *One of my talents is to share power. I've linked you to your Shadow. Her wolf is lending you her power.*

He could feel the dragon gliding silently overhead. Matt wouldn't interfere unless Juan was getting away from the ground party. Sascha was taking no chances of Raphael's puppet making it home alive.

The influx of power made the world come into sharp focus. Everything was more—sight, smell, and hearing. This had to be how a wolf shifter experienced the world.

When everything calmed down, he would make sure that Sheila and her wolf understood how grateful he was for the gift.

The two Nightshade moved to the center of the street. It was in the middle of the night, and they were far out from civilization. No one with sense would be out driving.

Juan raised his arms into the air, and red light spilled from his hands to form a half circle ten feet in diameter. "I call the challenge circle into existence."

Flashy bastard. Xavier formed his half circle of white light with just a thought. He dropped his cloak of darkness as the two halves of the circle met. There was a flash as the half-circles joined and formed a full circle.

Per the rules of challenge among the Nightshade, neither combatant could leave the circle until one was dead. If one tried to leave, the circle itself would prevent it. Which was why the challenge wasn't called often. Once committed, there was no going back.

"I call upon Hecate to seal the challenge circle and stop any who would interfere with your sacred challenge!" Xavier smiled as the circle flared, and light raised up over the pair to form a dome of protection.

Very few things could cross a challenge circle and live. And none of those things were present in this lonely part of the desert.

Juan gave Xavier a mocking salute before dropping into a fight-ready stance. Xavier just willed his fangs and claws to grow for his response. Within two seconds, he was sporting three-inch dagger like claws on each hand.

His opponent lashed out with a blast of pure power. Xavier instinctively threw up a barrier of power to deflect it. The blast bent the barrier slightly but didn't even come close to breaching it. It would take a stronger strike than that.

Instead of striking back with power, like Juan probably expected, Xavier rushed him physically and struck him in the face with a fist. Juan stumbled back, and Xavier followed with a series of punches and jabs that only allowed the interloper to defend himself.

Xavier continued pressing his attack, forcing Juan closer to the edge of the circle.

Juan realized his danger and kicked out at Xavier, forcing him to back up. The Cleveland Master dodged another rapid-fire kick, causing him to back away from the edge. He was waiting to use his telekinetic abilities until he saw a perfect opportunity.

The other Nightshade obviously had no compunction about using his unique abilities. He raised his hands up, and fire suddenly surrounded them.

Fuck! The bastard was a pyro. It was time to stop messing around and finish this challenge.

Juan flung his hand outward. A fireball formed and flew toward Xavier. He ducked it, rushing at the other Nightshade. Juan tried to counter by shoving at him, but Xavier dropped into a slide and slammed into his legs feet-first.

The other vampire flew slightly into the air and then slammed down onto the pavement face first. Xavier ended his slide and jumped up to face him.

Before Juan could correct himself, Xavier made a slashing motion with both hands. His telekinetic power lifted Juan and flung him hard into the dome wall. The vampire hit it and rebounded back to hit the pavement again. The fire surrounding his hands went out.

There was no drain like normal on his power. Xavier quickly checked, and it was like he barely touched his power source. He didn't waste time trying to figure out what was going on.

He made a slicing motion with his hand, and his power slashed across Juan's face. The Nightshade screamed as the power cut across one eye. Xavier followed that up with lifting the hapless Juan into the air.

"Put me down, you bastard!" The previous cockiness in the Nightshade was gone. For the first time since the encounter started, Xavier saw fear in him. Good, it probably dawned on him he was not the stronger Nightshade.

"I don't think so." Xavier started moving his hands like he was positioning a doll. Juan's body followed the motions until he was floating with arms out even with his shoulders and his legs spread.

Try as he might, Juan could not move from the position that Xavier had him in. And the pain from his ruined face kept him from focusing enough to use his power.

"You made the mistake and targeted my people." Xavier moved so he was now less than a foot away from the struggling Nightshade. "But your fatal error was going after my Shadow. See you in hell."

Lightning fast, Xavier reached out to grab Juan's head. With a quick snap, he broke the Nightshade's neck. He then released the body, and it dropped to the ground.

The dome wavered but didn't fade. Juan wasn't dead yet. A Nightshade wouldn't die from a broken neck, but it would take days and a lot of blood to heal. Something that Juan here wasn't going to get.

Xavier kneeled down beside the body and used his claws to rip his shirt off. He stared for a moment at the pale chest in the fitful light of the moon. Then he sliced into his chest with his claws, revealing the pumping heart. He reached in and ripped the heart from Juan's chest, then crushed it.

"May Hecate have mercy on your soul, because I sure won't."

Xavier watched as the dome dissolved with the death of Juan. The power that had been loaned to him from Sheila flowed back out of him. He now felt very drained from the fight.

His senses also returned to their normal state. The world was less bright, and his sense of smell had dimmed. Xavier knew he would forever treasure the trust that Sheila showed him. The hope that they could work things out surged within him.

"Xavier!" Brody came running up to the remains of the circle. "Are you hurt?"

He took a deep breath. His ribs protested the movement. "Damn, I didn't realize that he had connected with my ribs." He probed at one and winced in pain. "I think he broke a couple of my ribs."

The Alpha looked over at the remains of Xavier's opponent. "Well, you broke more than that on him." He toed the dead vampire. "Is he dead?"

"Yes. I tore out his heart." Xavier didn't feel like explaining that the circle would still be up if Juan were alive. "I hate to ask this, but can you take command? The challenge took it out of me."

"Of course." Brody touched his earpiece and started giving commands over it. He also called for one of the Nightshade to come over and guard Xavier.

The man who was to guard took one look at his Master and took over. "Sir, do you want to go back to the truck and drink some blood?"

Xavier shook his head sharply. "No. As soon as the house is clear, we're going in for Sheila." There was no way that he was going to wait in relative safety while others rescued his mate. The only reason that he wasn't heading first into the house was that he was too weak from the challenge with Juan.

"At least get under cover. We're going in." Brody turned and went back to where some of his men waited. Xavier and his guard disappeared into the shadows. They would go in after Brody gave the all-clear.

After they settled into their hiding space, Xavier attempted to reach out to Sheila. He cursed not having Bonded to her before this. If he had, he would be able to hear what she was thinking.

He touched her mind and got the impression that she was waiting for something. Hopefully, she wasn't near Dennis, but he knew that realistically, the bastard probably had her near him and would try to use her as a bargaining chip to escape.

There was no way that Dennis would be allowed to escape. He had a death sentence from both the Moon Council and the Nightshade Courts. Sascha had issued a kill-on-sight order as soon as she got word of Sheila's kidnapping.

It was important that they made the statement that to target a Shadow meant death.

# Chapter Twenty-Eight

S heila jerked a bit when her wolf slammed back into her body. The fight was over, and Xavier must have won. Her body filled with energy from her wolf's return.

"Fuck me!" snarled Dennis, turning away from the window. He walked over to Sheila and motioned for her to get up. "Let's go!"

Sheila tried to get up but stumbled. Dennis reached down and snatched her up. "I said get up, bitch!" His spittle hit her face as she tried to steady herself.

It took major effort for her not to show her satisfaction at his nerves. She was happy that it was his turn to be nervous. But she didn't let it show. A nervous Dennis could kill her just the same as the cocky Dennis. And being dead did not feature in her plans at all.

Dennis dragged her to the door, the goon following them. Sheila didn't resist being pulled, but she didn't hurry either. She purposely stumbled as they entered the hall.

That barely slowed her captor down. They trotted down the hall toward a staircase. The goon jumped in front of them and stopped Dennis from heading down. He took his gun out and slowly started down the stairs. After he got down to the bottom, he motioned for them to start down.

The Alpha didn't even look back at Sheila; he just tugged at her and started down. Sheila didn't pretend to stumble on the stairs. She didn't want to fall for real. As they descended the stairs, she could hear heavy footsteps racing through the house.

Her heart started beating fast. She might be free in a matter of moments. Her wolf was close to the surface. Sheila could feel her looking out through her eyes at the surroundings.

She looked down at Dennis's waist. He was packing a gun. Too bad it would be too much of a risk to grab it. Dennis would look so much better with a bullet hole in his head.

A crash in another part of the house caused Dennis to let her go and reach for his gun.

"Hello, Dennis." Brody's voice ran throughout the house. Sheila could see Dennis's shoulders tense up. She stopped moving on the stairs.

Dennis held up his gun and pointed silently to the right. The goon nodded and started down the hall to the left.

Sheila's muscles tensed. It looked as if she might have a chance to run back up the stairs. If she made it, she could barricade herself inside a room.

Before she could move an inch, Dennis turned to look at her. She nearly recoiled from his expression. He was cornered, and he knew it.

"This is your fault."

"Nah, fam. This is all on you," said Sheila calmly. Far calmer than she actually felt. Her muscles trembled as she stood looking down at her tormentor.

A yell echoed from the hall in the direction that the goon took before it was silenced. Well, Brody's people must have ended the goon's life. Sheila didn't even pretend to feel any pity for him.

"All of your men are dead." Brody's voice was much closer this time. He and his people were probably tracking them by scent. She and Dennis had to be throwing out enough pheromones to stink up the house.

"I'll kill the bitch here." Dennis's eyes kept darting between Sheila and the hallway. So far, no one appeared. But Sheila could now smell her Alpha, his power close.

Some strength flowed back into Sheila's body. She could tell it was coming via the Pack bond through Brody and the others in her Pack. She didn't dare try to focus too much on the bond, but she thought that there had to be at least twenty members of the Blackwood Pack around.

"And if you do, you won't walk out alive." This time, Brody's voice was soft and reasonable. And very close. If she had to estimate, he was probably in the next hallway over.

Dennis shifted his attention away from Sheila and held his gun out in front of him. "If you want to see her again, you'll let us walk out and leave. I'll drop her off somewhere, and you can grab her."

Sheila wondered if he actually thought that it would work like that. There was no way that Brody and his Pack would let him walk out the door alive. And if they were stupid enough to let him walk, the Nightshade would jump him and drain him dry.

There was a long silence before Brody's voice floated back. "That's not going to happen. Surrender and you'll go on trial with the Moon Council. Try to escape and I'll shoot you in the back as you run."

"If you don't get out of my way, I'll kill this stupid bitch here." Dennis raised his gun at the same time the other wolves arrived at the base of the stairs.

Time slowed down to a crawl for all those watching. Sheila jumped down the stairs as Dennis aimed the gun at her. She blurred into the form of her wolf mid-jump.

The wolf crashed into the Alpha. Both rolled into the hallway, causing those in the way to scatter to avoid being crushed. The others who hadn't dodged watched in helpless horror as the two tussled on the ground.

Sheila kept snapping and clawing at Dennis, preventing him from getting enough concentration to change forms. They fought tooth and nail for about thirty seconds before Sheila saw her chance.

She let him push her off him. Dennis was too far extended into the move and his neck was exposed. She darted in and tore his throat out. He let her go to clutch at his throat.

"Sheila! Back off!" Brody yelled, adding power to the command. She growled but followed her Alpha's command.

One of the Pack members got between her and Dennis. He walked to her, causing her to take a few steps away from the dying body. Sheila growled again, and the man laughed. "Calm down, warrior. You're safe now."

# Chapter Twenty-Nine

X avier walked beside the wolf shifter who was holding Sheila. She hadn't moved since she collapsed unconscious after she shifted back. They walked the distance back to the SUV so that they could wait for the others to finish in the house.

The sound of wings overhead caused both Xavier and the shifter to look up. It was Matt, landing near the SUVs. He changed back into his human form and met them at the vehicles.

"Is Sheila all right?" asked Matt as they got within easy speaking distance. He looked down at the bloody woman.

"Just exhausted. She's been through a lot with no food or water." Xavier opened the door so the wolf could set Sheila into the back seat.

The wolf grinned with pride. "She killed the Alpha Dennis in a fight."

Matt didn't appear to be surprised. But he was also satisfied. "You have a strong Shadow, Xavier. Make sure you treasure her."

Oh, Xavier had already planned on spending the rest of their long life together, making sure that Sheila knew she was treasured. And the members of his Court would have to accept it as well.

"I will. It's going to take some time to go through Dennis's home. You need to see what they find before the Council blocks us from seeing any of it."

"I know. Do you mind if one of your people stays until Sascha sends someone to monitor?" Matt looked back at the house in the in the distance. "I would stay, but the Council of the Moon could accuse the Dragon Council of getting involved."

Xavier nodded. "Of course. I'll have them look as well. If I know Brody, he's already contacted the Council, and they will have someone enroute."

He waited until Matt walked behind the building to transform into his dragon form before calling one of his men over. He quickly explained what needed to be done before he had the driver take him and Sheila back to the compound.

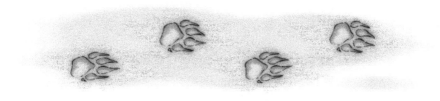

Matt invited Xavier and Brody's group back to Sascha's compound. While the invitation flattered Brody, Xavier expected it. Sascha would want to question them both.

If Brody had left Nevada before she had the chance to ask her questions, the Council of the Moon wouldn't allow it. His queen didn't have a great relationship with them at the best of times. Now that she had possession of the Crown of Ice, it was downright frosty.

When they arrived, Xavier had been escorted to a suite. He had refused all offers to carry Sheila up to their room. He cleaned and dressed Sheila without her waking at all. Matt had promised a healer from his Conclave would be up shortly to look at Sheila.

The healer arrived shortly after Xavier had taken a shower and dressed in fresh clothes. She had just flown in. Her hair was windblown, and she smelled of the desert air.

"Carla." Xavier leaned forward and kissed the air beside her cheeks. "I hadn't realized you were here in Las Vegas."

The petite, French healer smiled brightly at him. "Oui! The previous healer mated with a dragon from the Hawaii Conclave. So, when the Alpha here put out a call for a healer, I petitioned to come."

Xavier could sense there was more to the story, but he didn't pry. If the blue dragon wanted him to know, she would tell him.

She reached into the leather bag that was slung over her shoulders and pulled out a thermos. "Drink this."

He took the thermos carefully. Opening it, he smelled the coppery tang of blood. "I've already had some blood."

Carla waved her hand at him to drink. "I've added healing magic to it. The challenge took more out of you than you realize." She held his gaze with a stern one of her own. "Drink."

*I forgot that arguing with a healer is pointless.* Xavier took a drink of the blood.

"Let me look at my patient." Carla went over to the bed where Sheila lay sleeping. She set her bag down on the nightstand.

"Do you need me to help in any way?" asked Xavier.

Carla didn't even look at him before replying. "No. I'm just going to do a basic scan." She held her hands a few inches above Sheila's face.

Xavier could feel the power swirl around Carla but couldn't tell what she was doing with it. While the power that all Supernatural creatures had came from the same source, each race used it differently.

After a minute, Carla dropped her hands. "Your Shadow is suffering from exhaustion, dehydration, and hunger." She smiled at Xavier in reassurance. "Nothing that rest and food won't cure."

Relief nearly overcame Xavier. Sheila would be all right. "Will she wake soon?"

"Not for some hours yet. I want to get an IV setup to get her some fluids." Carla grabbed her bag and rifled through it until she pulled out a phone. She typed something on it and then put it back. "Sascha and Matt are expecting you in the library. I'll stay with Sheila for a while to make sure that she's settled."

He scowled briefly. There was no point in getting upset that his queen wanted to see him. Although all he wanted to do was stay with Sheila until she woke up.

Carla read the brief scowl accurately. "She won't be awake for hours. Take care of your business with the queen." She shooed him with her hands. "Go!"

"Xavier! It's been too long since you visited." Sascha rose from her chair where she had been reading. She glided to him and gave him a hug.

He returned her hug, amazed as always at the power and beauty that she possessed. Sascha was a very pale-skinned Nightshade with sable hair, deep blue eyes, and aquiline features. She was one of the oldest vampires in North America, and it was said that her line was descended from the Fae that called Russia home. Not too many knew her genuine history.

She was a powerful Magician in her own right. Supposedly, she had learned her craft from the most powerful Magicians that existed. Xavier thought it was true since she had strong political ties with the Magician's Council.

He let her go and smiled down at her. "I will have to get out here more often."

"Come sit! I know Andre keeps you busy with Cleveland." Sascha returned to her seat. Xavier took the one across from her.

Sitting across from Sascha brought back good times from his childhood when Andre would bring him to Las Vegas for Court visits. Sascha would tell him stories every evening before she had Court in this very library. Xavier just thought the stories were exciting tales she made up for him. It wasn't until later that he found out that she had been teaching him ancient Nightshade history.

Sascha had also given him the startup capital for Silver Enterprises when he graduated from the Nightshade Academy. She had been more of a mother figure to him than his own distant mother.

"Matt and the wolf alpha will be here shortly." She started tapping the brown leather of her chair with a blood-red fingernail. "I wanted to find out about Sheila and how the two of you are getting along."

# Chapter Thirty

Sheila woke feeling warm and safe for the first time in a long time. *Why was she so warm?* She opened her eyes, then closed them again.

The room was completely dark, but her senses confirmed she wasn't in the penthouse or her apartment. She struggled to open her eyes again.

The source of heat beside her shifted. Sheila forced her heavy eyelids to open before turning her head to look at the dark shape beside her.

"How are you feeling?" Xavier's voice rumbled in the darkness.

"Where are we? How are you here?" Her voice came out as a hoarse croak.

"We're in a room on Queen Sascha's estate." Xavier draped his arm over his waist. "Do you remember anything from the rescue?"

Memories of her time at Dennis's house flooded into her head. The memory of her wolf taking over to help her rip Dennis's throat out was the one that stood out the most. She could still remember the taste of his blood as it gushed into her mouth. Her stomach was threatening to revolt on her.

"Oh, my Goddess. I killed someone."

Xavier leapt out of bed, scooped her up, and carried her to the bathroom before she lost the contents of her stomach.

Minutes later, Xavier had her tucked back into bed beside him. She was so thankful that he was there. The last two days had been an absolute nightmare.

"Feeling better?" Xavier reached over and pushed her hair behind her ear.

Sheila's stomach wasn't threatening to revolt against her. She nodded and snuggled closer to him. "Thanks!"

"I'll always be here for you." Xavier put a finger under her chin and lifted it so that she was staring into his brown eyes. "Do you want to talk about it?"

For a long moment, Sheila stared into his eyes, basking in the warmth that she saw there. Those eyes let her see into him in a way that she hadn't before. The ruthless Master of the City was there, but that wasn't all.

Xavier, the vampire, was there too. The one who cared for her and would have her back in a way that no one else would. Why hadn't she seen that before? She probably hadn't seen it because she was too busy feeling sorry for herself.

She took a deep breath. "During the fight, three of Dennis's goons forced me away from the clearing. They then darted me with some sort of drug. I woke up as the plane was taking off from Cleveland."

Her love's arm tightened around her shoulder, but he didn't interrupt.

"Dennis gloated over catching me and made sure to tell me that an assassin would kill you that night. I wanted to bite his nose off, but I was too terrified to do anything since I was tied up." Sheila's voice shook as she remembered the terror that she felt at being Dennis's captive.

She continued telling Xavier what happened until they got to the fight. "We were cornered in the stairwell. Dennis was getting really desperate. And desperate wolves do stupid shit." Sheila paused once more before continuing. Xavier just let her take her time.

Images of Dennis raising his arm to point his gun at her assaulted her. "I had a split second to decide whether I wanted to live or die." She also had an epiphany in that fraction of a second.

Her life was precious, and she had too much to live for. There was no way she was going to let Dennis kill her when Xavier was waiting outside for her. It was her or him.

Sheila chose herself and her love for Xavier.

"I ripped his throat out." Tears started flowing down her cheeks again. "I would do it again. I should feel bad, but I don't!"

And that was the problem. She should feel terrible for taking a life. But she didn't. She was relieved that her nightmare with Dennis was finally over.

"It's alright. You did what you had to do," Xavier said soothingly. "I wish I could have killed him for you."

She looked up at him. "Shouldn't I feel bad though?"

Xavier kissed her lightly on the cheeks. "You should never take a life for pleasure. But in this case, no. If you didn't act, Dennis wouldn't have hesitated to take your life."

The hole that her emotions made deep in her heart closed from the combination of Xavier's words and presence. His nearness was like a balm to her soul, and she thanked the Moon Goddess that he was there.

"Thank you for coming to get me." Before he could respond, Sheila put her finger over his lips. "There was no doubt that you were coming for me." She smiled. "You are the first person who sees *me* and still cares."

"I understand."

Sheila could tell that he meant that.

"And I want you to know that I love you." Xavier snorted with laughter when Sheila sat upright.

She turned herself so that she faced him. Her sudden smile was so bright, it could light up the room. "You do?"

"Yes, I do."

His scent confirmed that he wasn't lying. Sheila's heart felt full to bursting. "I love you too!" She threw her arms around his neck and kissed him soundly.

They broke apart a minute later when Xavier pulled back. "I have something to give you." He reached over, opened the drawer of the nightstand, and pulled something out. It was a small, red velvet jewelry box.

"Here." Xavier handed the box to her.

The small box had a white ribbon bow on it. Sheila opened it and sharply inhaled when she saw what was inside. There was a beautiful ruby and diamond ring in it. The band was made of gold and the stones caught the light from the room.

"Thank you!" Tears of happiness formed in her eyes.

Xavier took the box from her and pulled the ring out before taking her hand in his to slide the ring on her finger. "Sheila Blackstone, will you do me the honor of becoming my Shadow?"

"Yes!" Her heart brimming with joy, Sheila kissed Xavier for all she was worth.

# Chapter Thirty-One

Sheila walked slowly down the street that held her parents' trailer. It was dusk, and the street was deserted. An occasional twitching curtain indicated she was being observed.

Unlike other homes in southern Nevada, none of the yards had any type of landscaping. No drought-hardy plants or even decorative rocks graced the yards. But there were bikes, old cars, and other objects all about. The entire trailer park just seemed down and out.

When she had awakened earlier in the day, she felt as if there was something that she needed to do to close the chapter on her life in Nevada. So, she asked Brody if someone from the Pack could escort her to her parents' trailer. Brody had looked at her with understanding and agreed.

A couple of hours later, all the Pack members who had come to Las Vegas were waiting for her at the SUVs. It took everything she had not to break down crying. Their act showed her what a caring Pack would do for a member.

They now waited for her at the end of the block. Another SUV pulled up alongside the others, and a couple of other figures exited the vehicle.

She stopped in front of the house. There was a light shining through the front window. Who was in the house?

The door opened, and her brother Dave stood in the doorframe. He didn't look surprised to see her. "Sheila!"

Sheila didn't move as her brother left the house and walked up to her. Dave was wearing dirty clothing and didn't look as if he had bathed in a week. She could feel the Pack watching the pair of them from the SUVs.

Dave tried to give her a hug, but Sheila stepped back. Her nose wrinkled from his rank smell. "When did you get back into town?" he asked casually. Something about him didn't smell right. And didn't sit right with her, either.

"Dennis kidnapped me from Cleveland and brought me back here."

"The rumors are flying around that someone killed him." Dave stared into her face intently. He was nearly vibrating with nervous energy. "How did you escape?"

It didn't seem like a good idea to tell him that she was the one who killed Dennis. He might have friends that would want revenge for his death. Xavier and Brody decided to let the rumors suggest that Brody killed him. After all, Dennis had kidnapped one of Brody's Pack. "He was killed during the rescue."

"Is it true that you've mated with the Master of Cleveland?" Dave's eyes gleamed with greed.

Sheila's heart sank. "I haven't mated with him. I'm his Shadow. How did you hear about it?"

"Rumors. All the Underworld has been buzzing how a wolf shifter mated with Xavier Silversbane." Dave starting smiling, his avarice showing. "He's a freaking billionaire. You hit the jackpot!"

"I have not hit the jackpot. His money is not my money." Sheila wished she had never come back to her parents' house. All of Xavier's suspicions about her brother were proving to be accurate.

Dave ignored her statement and kept right on talking. "I'm going to need around $100k to pay off my bookie."

"What?! I'm not asking Xavier for that kind of money." *Was he insane? On what planet did Dave think Xavier would give her that much cash?* "How did you get that deep in debt?"

"I had a streak of bad luck at the tables." Dave looked down at the diamond and ruby ring she wore on her hand, the one that Xavier had given her the night before, after they had kissed. "If you think it will take a while, you can give me that ring. I can get at least ten grand for it."

She held up her hand in exasperation. "I'm not giving you my ring or any money!" This was getting ludicrous. Her brother didn't seem to care about her at all. Sheila wondered if he ever loved her.

Her words must have finally punctured the bubble that Dave was in. His face twisted in a rictus of rage. "If it wasn't for me warning you about Dennis, you wouldn't have your fancy Nightshade. You owe me."

"I don't owe you a thing."

Dave barked a laugh. The scent of desperation overlaid the body odor wafting from him. "I'm in debt because of you. I was trying to win the money to come to Cleveland. Dennis offered to pay off my debt if I told him where you were. Instead, he sold the debt to another bookie."

His words hit her, shattering the love that she had for him. Her own brother sold her out for money. He threw her to the demon wolves to save his own hide. She didn't know this wolf who stood in front of her.

"How did you know I was in Cleveland?" Sheila hadn't known that she would end up there. So how in the hell did Dave know she had landed there?

"There was a tracker in your go bag. Dad put it there when he was afraid you'd ditch us some years back."

Just when she thought that she'd heard it all. Her dad tracked her? She didn't want to hear anything else from her brother. It was time to go.

Sheila turned to walk away when Dave grabbed her shoulder. Then, he was pushed away from her.

Xavier stood beside her. Sheila looked up at him in surprise. He had still been at the estate when they left.

"I suggest you keep your hands off Sheila." The chill in Xavier's voice could freeze water in a glass.

Her brother looked sullenly at Xavier. "You're gonna choose him over me?"

Reaching out her hand, she grabbed Xavier's in hers. "Dave, you chose money over me." She squeezed Xavier's hand. "For the first time, I'm finally choosing my own destiny."

Dave took a step toward her but stopped when Xavier's eyes started glowing yellow and his fangs descended. Then he looked past them at the Pack, who started approaching. "Who are the goons?"

Sheila looked back over her shoulder and smiled. "Members of my Pack from Cleveland."

"I can't believe this! Don't you have any loyalty to our family? You sold out to a Pack." Dave spat on the ground. "Give me the ring, and I'll think about forgiving you."

And pigs would fly. She didn't know her brother anymore. The person in front of her was a stranger. "Goodbye, Dave." Sheila looked up at Xavier. "We need to head back so that we can plan our Bonding ceremony."

# Chapter Thirty-Two

All anyone in the Supernatural world could talk about was the Bonding ceremony between Xavier and Sheila. Xavier pulled out all the stops on the festivities leading up to it. Since Sascha announced she was officiating it, he invited all the power brokers in the Supernatural world.

That had involved a lot of coordination between the heads of the different races. Sheila took the lead there. Within a few days of their return to Cleveland, she had contacted most of the Shadows and seconds in command to work out the specifics of so many Supernaturals being in one city.

She had done such an outstanding job that Sascha had jokingly told Xavier that she was considering reassigning the two of them to her Court. He had the feeling that she wasn't joking. He had been on pins and needles that Sascha would take his city from him and make them move to Las Vegas.

Finally, Matt told him he convinced the Queen to let them remain in Cleveland.

The day of their Bonding finally arrived.

"Here." Lord Andre Silversbane of the Midwest handed his cousin a wine glass.

Xavier took the wineglass. It was filled with blood wine. From the smell, it was a chardonnay.

"Where did you get this? I don't have any bloodwine in the suite." He took a sip and felt the jolt from the blood inside.

Andre laughed. Well, it only being just the two of them in the penthouse, the Lord was free to express his emotions. "It's part of Simone and Matt's gift to you. A dozen bottles of blood were made with their blood."

Xavier felt his eyebrows raise nearly to his hairline. "I must remember to thank them." He took another appreciative sip. It was excellent. "How in the world did they pull it off so fast? I'm still on the waiting list from two years ago."

"Well, the winemaker is a special friend of Matt's." Andre couldn't keep the grin off his face.

"I'll just have to tell Matt that I appreciate him sacrificing his body for the gift." Everyone among the Nightshade Courts knew Matt loved sex. He didn't care if his partner was male or female.

It always amazed Xavier that Matt and Sascha were so perfect as a Bonded pair. The Queen and her Shadow were not a love match. Their relationship was purely based on friendship and respect.

The phone in Andre's pants pocket went off. He pulled it out and answered it. "We're on our way."

Nervousness and pride swelled in Xavier's chest. He was about to complete the Bonding ceremony with his beautiful wolf. Everything that led up to this moment flashed through him.

Although the road up to this point had been really rough, it had been worth it.

He drained the wine glass and set it down on the coffee table. "Let's go."

# Chapter Thirty-Three

S heila sat still as the makeup artist performed her magic on her face.
She had been in another apartment in the Tower since midday. And
she hadn't been alone. Penny, Lena, Andre's Shadow Simone, and a few
others had been with her, helping her to prepare.

First, she had to take a ritual bath with salts and oils given to her by
a priest of Hecate. That was followed by the priest praying over her for
two hours while she lay on a bed. Sheila didn't remember what the prayers
contained. From the moment the first word left his lips, she had been in a
partial daze.

Now, the small group in the apartment was helping her put the final
touches of her outfit together. She and Penny had put their heads together
to go all out for the ceremony.

"I wish I had the confidence to pull off your outfit," said Simone as the
makeup artist stepped back. The dragon whistled as Sheila turned to look
at her. "Look at you!"

Sheila's eyes had been done up in white eyeshadow with dramatic cat's
eye. The tips of the eyeliner winged up fairly high on her face. Her lips
were painted with white lipstick. In contrast to the complicated makeup,
her hair had been pressed straight and lay about her shoulders. The choice
in makeup colors was done on purpose to highlight her white outfit.

The inspiration for the outfit came from Isabella Rossellini's costume in *Death Becomes Her*. Her top was made of white beads and crystal charms of various sizes that formed a large necklace that covered her neck and breasts. Since Sheila was noticeably larger in the breasts than the movie character, there was a beaded strap that went across her back to keep the necklace from shifting as much.

The skirt was white velvet that dipped low on her waist and went down to her ankles. There was a slit that went up to her thigh that showed her legs when she walked. In deference to the fact that her necklace top was very heavy and wouldn't take much to lose, she wore simple, white ballerina flats.

After all, it wouldn't do to trip in front of the assembled audience.

Sheila had initially wanted her outfit in a different color, but Penny informed her that all Shadows wore white during their Bonding ceremony. When she had asked the shop owner why, Penny had given her a particularly chilling answer. "So the blood shows, of course."

No matter how much Sheila had asked about the ceremony after that, no one in the Tower would tell her. The lack of information didn't help Sheila's nervousness about the ceremony one bit.

"I lived my life previously just trying to blend in so I wouldn't be noticed." Sheila stood and stretched. She had been in that chair for nearly an hour. "Since I can't go that route being Xavier's shadow, I decided I would go in the opposite direction."

"Lady Silversbane, remind me to show you the pictures of what she wore to the gala," said Penny from the other side of the room. The shop keeper was looking through jewelry options that had been couriered to the Tower earlier in the day.

Sheila walked over to Penny and looked at what she had displayed on the table. She noticed a wide bracelet made up of crystals. She pointed to it. "How about that one?"

Penny picked it up and held it against her wrist. "Yes. This will work. And Henri sent a second matching bracelet."

There was a stir as Lena walked into the room. She was munching on an apple from the kitchen. "What about rings?"

"No rings. The bling on the fingernails is enough." Penny made a moue of distaste.

There had been a long discussion about her nails. Sheila wanted long acrylic nails with designs and bling. Penny kept arguing for natural nails done with a simple French manicure. Sheila won out and had her nails done in blood red with crystals and designs in silver.

She held out her arms, and Penny snapped both bracelets onto her arms. "Where's the full-length mirror? I want to see the full outfit."

"It's out in the living room." Lena moved out of the doorway so that Sheila could exit the room.

In the living room of the small apartment, a tall mirror had been propped up against the wall. Sheila went and stood in front of it. She smiled at the sight she presented.

No one present at the ceremony would mistake her for a wallflower. Everyone would know that the new Lady of Cleveland was going to be fierce and in their face.

Hopefully, she would see Xavier's jaw drop. The Nightshade had trouble keeping his hands to himself at the best of times. She would make sure that he was tempted all night long.

"Girl, Xavier is going to have trouble keeping his hands to himself," said Lena, coming up beside her.

"I think that's the point." Simone exited the room. "All the Silversbane line is going to worship the ground you walk on."

Sheila turned from the mirror and frowned at the dragon shifter. "Why?"

Simone gave her a cheeky grin. "Did you know that the Silversbane line is descended from an Incubus?"

"No." To be honest, Sheila knew little about the various Nightshade lines. She would have to rectify that after the excitement from the Bonding ceremony died down.

"Yes. Most of them will feed off the sexual tension in the room." Simone eyed her carefully. "You didn't notice that Xavier had a higher-than-normal sex drive when it came to you?"

She could feel a flush creeping up her neck. "Well... I'm a wolf, and we love sex... So, no." Honestly, she thought the amount of sex they had was normal.

Both Lena and Simone broke into gales of laughter. It was a moment before Simone calmed down enough to speak again. "Every time the two of you have sex, he gets an energy boost from it. That's the Incubi part of his bloodline."

A cell phone rang in the bedroom. All three women heard Penny answer it. Then, the Nightshade stuck her head into the room. "It's time."

# Chapter Thirty-Four

Tim was standing outside of the ballroom when Sheila arrived, escorted by Penny, Lena, and Simone. He gave her a wink as he opened the door for the other three ladies to enter.

"Congratulations, Sheila," he said with quiet dignity.

"Thank you, Tim. Do you think we have to wait long?" Sheila twitched her skirts to settle them about her legs.

"Nah. I just have to give the ladies enough time to settle in their seats." He cracked the door open and peeked in. "In fact, I think they are ready for you."

Sheila took a moment to make sure that her top hadn't moved. After all, this wasn't a time to give everyone a show. Then, she took a deep breath and nodded at Tim. The guard gave her an encouraging smile and then opened the door for her.

Inside, the crowd immediately quieted. The silence was so thick that she thought everyone present in the room could hear her heart thumping wildly in her chest.

The inside of the ballroom was filled with rows of chairs divided by a central walkway. The walkway had a very long, crimson runner that was inlaid with silver abstract. At the head of the room was a long table that was completely covered by a crimson, velvet cloth. Behind that were one grand throne-like chair and two slightly less grand chairs on either side of it.

In the middle chair sat Queen Sascha, with Lord Andre on her left and Xavier on her right. All three were stylishly dressed in black leather. The queen was in a skintight black leather dress, and the two men were in leather pants with tailored, white silk shirts.

Sheila had to hold back a giggle as she imagined the queen struggling to get into that dress.

*You and Matt find the strangest things funny.*

She nearly died of embarrassment when Sascha looked directly at her and winked.

The Lord of the Midwest stood up, and every eye in the room turned towards him. "Sheila Davis of the Blackwood Pack, approach the altar."

From his seat beside Sascha, Xavier sat watching her with an impassive expression. His eyes, however, spoke of the passion that he held inside. Sheila locked eyes with him briefly and then started forward.

As she passed the members of the audience, she could hear their low comments about her daring outfit. Most approved, but there were a few stuffy sorts muttering about indecency. Sheila ignored those comments. As long as Xavier loved the outfit, the rest could go take a long hike off a short cliff.

Sheila stopped in front of the altar. She looked down at the silk cloth that covered it. There were runes stitched into the cloth with gold thread. She looked a little more closely at it and wondered if the thread was actually gold. If so, that cloth was worth more than her truck.

"Do you come to this bonding of your own free will?" Andre's question drew her attention back to him.

"Yes."

"Then please lie on the altar."

Thanking the gods that she wore ballet flats, Sheila hopped lightly up and landed rump first on top of the altar. She swung her legs up onto the table and then lay back. *Oh gods, I'm giving everyone side-boob shots.*

*Trust me, all the men in here are wishing you were theirs,* thought Xavier. *I'm sure that I'm being called all sorts of lucky bastard right now.*

Sascha stood and walked over to the altar while Andre resumed his seat.

From the planning, she knew that there were at least three hundred watching the ceremony.

"Let everyone present bear witness to the joining of Xavier Silversbane and Sheila Blackstone in the eyes of the Goddess Hecate." Sascha moved so that she was standing at Sheila's head. She held her hands over Sheila's upper body.

"When the spell is complete, there will be one where there was once two. Xavier and Sheila's souls will combine, and the two shall live and die as one."

The lights in the room dimmed, and Sascha's hands started glowing brightly. She began chanting in what Sheila thought was Latin.

The air around Sheila grew warm, and Sascha's voice receded until it sounded as if she were down a long hallway. Sheila quickly became uncomfortable as sweat formed on her forehead. Looking around, it seemed as if Xavier was the only other person in the room affected.

His eyes were glowing yellow. They were bright in the room's dimness. He locked gazes with her and walked over to the altar to stand by her side.

The power in the room built as Sascha's chant continued. It flowed back and forth between them. It was so strong that Sheila swore she could actually see it. The more that the power arced between herself and Xavier, the stronger it became.

Then, when it was almost too much to bear, Sascha stopped chanting. She lifted her hands above her head. They were glowing almost too brightly for one to look at.

The entire room held its breath. For a long moment, no one moved. Then, Sascha and Xavier moved at the same time. The Queen brought her hands down sharply, while Xavier struck at Sheila like a serpent.

He leaned over and bit down with his fangs at the junction of Sheila's neck and shoulder.

Sheila screamed, power bursting over her as Xaiver's fangs sank deep into her skin. Both the bite and power hurt like hell for an instant before she fainted.

"Damn, what happened?" Sheila groaned as she opened her eyes. She realized she was in the master bedroom of the penthouse. Looking down, she noticed she didn't have any clothes on.

*Can't you figure it out?*

Xavier's thought was just as clear as if he spoke aloud. But he wasn't in the room with her. Then, Sheila realized she could feel his amusement.

"We're bonded?" This time, her voice was a whisper. *The ceremony had worked*!

"Yes, love, we are." Her sexy vampire walked into the room carrying a tray with a covered dish of food. She could smell the appetizing aroma of fried chicken and mashed potatoes. He wore nothing but a pair of silk boxers.

Sheila eagerly sat up as he sat the tray on the dresser. While the food smelled good, she wanted the vampire carrying it. As her eyes roamed down the length of his body, she could see a certain piece of his anatomy rising in his boxers.

His chuckle caused her to look back up at his face. He was grinning at her.

"What?" she demanded.

"Nothing, my love. I'm just happy to see you."

She froze at his words. His true feelings for her slid through their bond, and her heart beat faster in response. *My love.* Sheila never thought that someone would say those words to her and mean it.

She jumped out of bed and raced over to him. Xavier barely had enough time to catch her as she flung herself into his arms. He laughed as she rained kisses down all over his face. "What's this about?"

"I love you!" Sheila couldn't get anything else out past the lump in her throat and the tears in her eyes. She had to switch over to mind speech. *You're the first person to ever call me my love.*

*I will call you that for the rest of our lives. I love you, Sheila Silversbane.*

*I love you, Xavier Silversbane.*

# About Danni Williams

If you want to be added to my newsletter to hear about my latest releases click here. You'll get a free story.

Danni Williams is an avid reader of romance and fantasy books. Working with her trusty pooch Luci, she tries to bring to life the stories that others would like to read about.

Website: http://danniwilliamsauthor.com

# Also By

## Shadow's Debt

**Dragon shifter Simone just wants to be left alone. But a debt owed by her father to vampire lord Andre Silversbane will disrupt Simone's future. Add to that a crazy vampire King who thinks Simone is the key to a major artifact and it will be all that she can do to stay alive.**

Simone is happily anticipating starting a new life in Chicago when life drops a bombshell on her. Her father owes vampire lord Andre Silversbane a debt and has given her to him.

Now Simone has to learn to survive among the Nightshade vampires as the new Lady Silversbane. And, survive a plot by the Mad King Rapheal, who wants her to retrieve an artifact that should remain hidden.

When tragedy strikes, Simone will have to make a decision that will change the world as she knows it or destroy it.

## Shadow's Doubt

**Dragon shifter Simone just wants to be left alone. But a debt owed by her father to vampire lord Andre Silversbane will disrupt Simone's future. Add to that a crazy vampire King who thinks Simone is the key to a major artifact and it will be all that she can do to stay alive.**

Simone is happily anticipating starting a new life in Chicago when life drops a bombshell on her. Her father owes vampire lord Andre Silversbane a debt and has given her to him.

Now Simone has to learn to survive among the Nightshade vampires as the new Lady Silversbane. And, survive a plot by the Mad King Rapheal, who wants her to retrieve an artifact that should remain hidden.

When tragedy strikes, Simone will have to make a decision that will change the world as she knows it or destroy it.

**Kindle Vella**


The Southern Cardinal

Talsia Dacian is a princess who is in exile due to the actions of her parents. Little does anyone know she's also the fabled Southern Cardinal, one of the four women who are rumored to be able to open the Gates of Hell and release the King of Hell from his thousand-year prison sentence. Follow the tale of her rise to power in the Southern Empire and that of her enemies whose sole mission is to send her to Hell so that she can be used to free the King of Hell and his four Lords.

Milton Keynes UK
Ingram Content Group UK Ltd.
UKHW040643040923
428018UK00001B/205